ROCK
Him

ROCK
Him

RACHEL CROSS
Author of *Rock Her* and *Spiraling*

CRIMSON
ROMANCE

F+W Media, Inc.

Published by Crimson Romance
an imprint of F+W Media, Inc.
10151 Carver Road, Suite 200
Blue Ash, OH 45242. U.S.A.
www.crimsonromance.com

ISBN 10: 1-4405-7926-1
ISBN 13: 978-1-4405-7926-4
eISBN 10: 1-4405-7269-0
eISBN 13: 978-1-4405-7269-2

Printed in the United States of America.

10 9 8 7 6 5 4 3 2 1

Cover design by Erin Alexander and Jessica Pooler.
Cover images © 123rf.com.

This book is available at quantity discounts for bulk purchases.
For information, please call 1-800-289-0963.

Dedication

For my girls

Acknowledgments

Many thanks to those who read and critiqued: Chris, Brona, Selena Laurence, Debra Kayn, Monica Tillery, Nicola, Stacie, Holly, Kristi, Gina, and Daniel.

Thanks to my editors: Jennifer Lawler, Tara Gelsomino, Jess Verdi, and a special thanks to developmental editor extraordinaire, Julie Sturgeon.

Finally, thanks to Kim, who shared her experiences.

Chapter 1

Asher Lowe lay atop his buttery-soft, Egyptian cotton sheets, sandwiched between two women. The brunette on his right snored delicately into the pillow, exposing a booty so spectacular it was said to be insured by Lloyd's of London. Last year's Miss November, a stacked, all-natural blonde, was curled up to his left, hogging the covers.

Clubbing most of the night and living out every man's fantasy into the wee hours was easier ten years ago. Well, the recovery from the all-nighters was certainly easier back then. The part in bed was easier then. Getting women into bed? Thanks to money, a wall full of platinum albums, and a couple of Grammys, that part was easier now.

Asher lifted his head and immediately regretted it. His head throbbed from all the damn Hennessy. Would he *ever* learn not to drink with rappers?

He glanced at the clock on the nightstand and did a double take. Eight A.M.? Why on earth was he up so early?

Bzzz.

Asher cringed. The headache reached nightmarish proportions and nausea rushed up as he broke out in a cold sweat.

More buzzing. What was that? Had some device been left on?

He sat up gingerly, moving to his knees, swallowing back bile, careful not to disturb either of the bed's occupants. The brunette stirred and he froze. He didn't have it in him for round three. Hell, he wasn't sure he had it in him to make it to the bathroom.

Asher's gaze swept the floor. Strewn about the plush, cream carpet was an assortment of satin underthings, an empty box of condoms, a pair of black thigh-high boots and a lacy, red thong. La Perla, by the looks of it. No vibrating paraphernalia.

He frowned. More buzzing. Coming from the corner of the room.

He inched his way to the bottom of the bed and stood. A wave of dizziness swept through him and he rested his hands on naked thighs, biting back a moan. Things were way worse vertical. Getting back to sleep would be impossible until he turned off whatever it was.

He spied his phone on the dresser, the telltale light coming on as the insistent noise started again. His brows went up. His phone? Who the hell would be calling at the crack of dawn? Must be a wrong number.

Only a handful of people even had his private cell number, and not one of them would call before noon.

The brunette mumbled something. Snagging his phone, he hustled to the bathroom. He put the phone down and rifled through the cabinets in search of some kind of hangover remedy. He tried a sip of water with a pink-stuff chaser. God. He had been here countless times over the years and it was never worth it.

Examining his reflection in the mirror, he saw the lines that marked years of exposure to the California sun and the inexorable march to forty. Bags and circles highlighted bloodshot eyes. Leaning against the vanity countertop, he cast a glance over his shoulder at the bathroom. Why were there towels all over the floor and a bottle of bubbles overturned, leaking clear goo—?

Oh yeah. The two in his bed had wanted to play in his hot tub–size bathtub.

His phone vibrated on the counter and he picked it up to stare blearily at the display. Six missed calls and six voice-mail messages from a familiar Vegas number.

Asher's mouth twisted. His father knew his cell number? Interesting. Finishing in the bathroom, he stumbled out to the bedroom where he hauled on last night's jeans. Shutting the door carefully behind him, he padded to the kitchen.

Dealing with Sterling Lowe would require coffee—in vast quantities.

He set the phone on the counter and pulled out the beans. The phone vibrated again. With a glare that renewed the throbbing in his head, he picked it up.

"Yeah?" he drawled.

"Asher." His father's voice was raspy.

Asher tensed.

Sterling Lowe drew a ragged breath. "Asher…I…I don't know how to tell you this. I…I hate to do it on the phone…"

His hand clenched into a fist; a cold, hard knot formed in his stomach. "Are you sick?"

"It's Delilah."

Delilah—Dee—Asher's half-sister.

His body grew cold. The hair on the back of his neck stood up. "What?" he whispered.

His father choked back tears, voice rough. "She was killed by a drunk driver in a head-on."

Asher collapsed onto a barstool.

"Ella?" he asked.

"She's here. I have her this weekend. Dee…Dee had a girls' weekend…I…haven't told Ella. I don't know what to do."

Some part of Asher could not believe his father had said that. Sterling Lowe always knew exactly what to do, or at least thought he did.

His father took a deep breath. "Can you come?"

"Of course." He gritted his teeth. He loved Dee. God knows he had been a better brother to her than Sterling had been a father. It was on the tip of his tongue to say something caustic when he heard a muffled sound. Asher pulled the phone from his ear and stared at it. Through all the divorces, the battles, in thirty-seven years, he had never heard his father weep. He put the phone back to his ear. "I'll be there as soon as I can."

"The jet is fueled up and ready at LAX. I sent a car—"

"I'm on my way."

"Wait. Asher?"

"Yes?"

"What do I tell," his voice was thick with tears, "Ella?"

"Can you wait until I get there?" He knew exactly who to call. The older man let out a long, relieved sigh. "Okay. Dee wasn't supposed to pick her up until later today."

"I'll see you soon."

Ella. With no father in the picture, what would happen to her?

His lips tightened and his hands formed fists. He'd be damned if he let his father ruin another childhood.

Asher hung up the phone and dialed Justin. He had been Asher's assistant for ten years. Next to Dee, Justin Montoya was the closest thing to family he had.

"*Asher*? What the hell? It's eight—"

"I know." He managed to speak through a throat half closed by unshed tears. "It's Dee." He gritted his teeth against a wave of grief, afraid if he said the words they would become true. "She was killed in a car accident in Vegas this morning."

"What? *Oh God*, Asher, not Dee—"

"I need to go," he interrupted before the sympathy in his friend's voice made him lose the slim bit of control he had left. "The plane is waiting. Do I have a bag packed somewhere?"

"Hall closet. What about Ella?"

"She's okay. She's with my dad." A thump from upstairs made him squeeze his eyes shut in frustration. "Listen, there's a couple of girls here. Can you—"

"I got it covered man, you just go."

"Thanks," he said.

Ten minutes later, the car arrived and Asher's hands had finally stopped shaking. Memories of his younger sister flashed before him. Ruthlessly, he pushed them away. He sent a group text to a handful of friends.

Dee killed in car accident. Headed to Vegas.

Better they hear it from him than from the news.

He put his bag in the trunk of the long, sleek, black limousine, nodded his thanks to the driver holding the door open, and climbed into the rear seat.

Ella.

Delilah had become pregnant with Ella in her mid-twenties when she was still thoroughly enmeshed in partying with other children of the ultra-rich. It was a scene Asher avoided. A scene he tried unsuccessfully to extricate his sister from.

Knowing Dee's crowd during that time, he was pretty sure the men she hung out with would either be horrified by the idea of becoming a daddy or thrilled for all the wrong reasons. Knocking up the daughter of one of the richest men in America had its advantages.

Asher had asked once, gently, about the father and Delilah told him she didn't know. He left it alone. Having a baby changed Dee. She had renewed purpose and vitality; being a mom and a good mom was everything to her.

He made the call to Kate Sawyer, wife of his best friend, Alec. Kate was a nurse and ran a foundation for terminally ill parents with dependent children. She and her sister had lost their mother at a young age. If anyone could answer questions about how to deal with Ella and grief, it was Kate.

He filled Kate in on the events of the morning, forcing the words out through numb lips.

"Oh, no, Asher." Her breath hitched.

"I've got to get on a plane in a few minutes, and when I get there I need to know what to tell Ella."

"Oh Asher," her voice shook, "I'm so sorry. I can't imagine what you're going through."

Asher heard Alec in the background, asking questions.

Kate shushed him. "What is Ella now? Five? Six?"

"Five."

Kate sighed. "The first thing you need to know is that her understanding of death will be limited."

"What does that mean?"

"Understanding death is a process at that age. She'll only understand what her mother's death means as she gets older."

"I'm not following you, Kate." Asher's control was slipping and he knew he sounded impatient.

"You need to explain to her in very simple terms that her mother died. She'll need to be told that death is nothing like sleep, and that her mom is not coming back. She'll cry and grieve but…it'll take time. Even once you think she understands, she will probably ask for her. Sometimes it takes months or longer for a child that age to grasp that Mom isn't coming back."

Oh God. She was going to be asking when Delilah would be *back*? He fought another upwelling of grief mixed with acute nausea.

"Children can also think something they've done or haven't done may have caused the death…"

"*What?*" he ground out through a stiff jaw. "That's insane."

"Asher, they don't think like we do. They aren't mini-adults. She'll need constant, patient reassurance. There are therapists who can help with this. I know a few excellent ones in L.A. I'll call this morning if you like."

"God. Yes. Thanks, Kate."

There was a long pause.

"Asher?"

"Yeah?"

Kate waded in. "We're here for you. Anything you need. Anything. Help. Visits. We loved Dee. You know we love you and Ella. And we understand your feelings toward your father."

Only a handful of people knew about his conflict-ridden relationship with his father; Sterling and Asher put on a good front in public.

He loved Ella because she was his sister's kid, but he had no interest in kids of his own. None at all. Not now at any rate. But Ella? My God. And his dad? No fucking way. He would not have her grow up the way he and Dee had, in a fractured family with a distant, disinterested parent. He would get the best people. He could set her up with a full-time nanny, the best schools. *He* could figure it out, not his dad.

Asher swallowed convulsively. "I know, Kate."

"We'll see you in a few hours; we'll be flying in from Cielito."

"See you in Vegas." Asher disconnected the phone and buried his face in his hands, finally giving in to grief.

Chapter 2

The limo glided through the wrought iron gates and up to Sterling's estate. Asher's lip curled into a sneer. The twenty-million-dollar mansion jutted into the cloudless sky like a child's metal dump truck left upended in a sandbox. The modern exterior was all hard angles and sharp lines.

He didn't see the appeal—not in the stark house or the desiccated landscape. As far back as Asher could remember, when his old man wasn't working, he was either at the country club, the nearest casino, or on vacation with a wife or girlfriend. Anywhere but home with his kids. Sterling could live wherever the hell he wanted, but Ella didn't belong here. A wide limestone path sliced the yard and ascended to a double-door entry. Terraced retaining walls flanked the steps and outlined shrub-strewn patches of gravel filled with spiky yucca and sharp-edged palms. Hell, a child wouldn't even be *safe* here.

The limo stopped. He grabbed his bag from the seat and got out without waiting for the driver. Asher waved a dismissal, and the driver got back in the car and put it in gear, leaving him standing in the brutal mid-morning sun. He groaned and squeezed his eyes shut, fumbling his sunglasses into place as he tried to blink away the headache that threatened to re-emerge.

During the hour-long flight to Vegas, his hangover had dissipated enough for him to pull himself together and contact his lawyer. Once things were moving on the legal front, he'd skimmed the information Kate had e-mailed.

Jesus, how did anyone tell a five-year-old such devastating news? It was going to be the hardest thing he'd ever done.

He climbed the steps two at a time and rang the bell. Rubbing a hand over his unshaven jaw, he realized he probably looked as bad as he felt. His jeans had an unidentifiable stain on one knee, and his oldest Metallica tee was wrinkled from spending last night balled up in a corner of his bedroom. The sickly stench of stale booze and sex oozed from his pores in the arid heat. Nothing like living down to the old man's expectations.

Sterling answered, eyes red-rimmed from weeping, his face ashen under his golfer's tan. "Asher." His father took a half step toward him through the doorway.

Asher took a step back.

Sterling Lowe sighed and pushed the door further open behind him. "Come on in."

Asher walked into the house, closed the front door and followed his father to the living room.

"So, what happened?" Asher asked.

"She was on her way home from a girls' night, a weekend actually. She had a drink or two early, but her blood alcohol was nil. She rarely drank anymore. No drugs. Nothing. You know she got away from all that before she had Ella."

Asher nodded.

"Some drunk crossed the line and hit her, head-on. They tell me she was killed instantly." Sterling rubbed his unshaven face.

"Driver still alive?"

"Of course, and it wasn't his first offense. He'll be in prison for a long time."

"So, Ella's been here a few days?"

"Yeah. I have her here as often as I can, which isn't often enough. I've become really close to both of them," Sterling said. "You may think it's too little, too late."

Asher shrugged, and crossed the room to the window where he studied the landscape. He gritted his teeth. All the feelings he had ferociously quashed were leaking through.

"I'm sorry, son. I know I was a lousy—"

Nausea rose up, bringing his past with it. He turned away from the window and gave his father a look through narrowed eyes. "Now's not the time."

He was the only child now, the only heir. No matter. He had dashed his father's dreams for a family succession of the business more than fifteen years ago. About the time Sterling had thrown his considerable weight around, leaning on people to cancel Spade's early gigs. Luckily, Canadian promoters had balls, or who knows if his band would have ever made it. It had occurred to him on the flight that Sterling might want to mend fences with his sole surviving offspring. His lips twisted. Dear old Dad wouldn't feel that way for long, not after the lawyers arrived. Asher hadn't been as close to Dee in the last year or two, and he laid that directly at his father's door. Dee's endless efforts to bring about reconciliation between the two had caused a growing rift. His sister was short on memory and long on forgiveness. Asher was hanging on by a thread. He would deal with the yawning pit of howling rage and despair later. After they told Ella.

Sterling walked over to the far side of the room and poured an amber-colored liquid from the crystal decanter on the sideboard. He offered it to Asher. "Hair of the dog?"

Asher stiffened. So his father had noticed. Not surprising. The hangover had barely ebbed, but he was not a proponent of that remedy. That path led to doom. "God, no." Asher walked over to the couch while his father settled himself into a straight-backed chair with his drink. "Where's Ella?"

"In the pool. The housekeeper is watching her for a bit while we talk."

Asher ran a trembling hand through his hair. "So, listen, I talked to my friend, a nurse who deals a lot with grieving families;

she's an expert with this kind of thing. I gotta tell you, Sterling, it's going to be bad. Real bad."

"I could've told you that," his father replied shakily and took a healthy swallow of the Scotch.

Asher relayed what Kate had told him about the way five-year-olds handle death. Then he dropped his bombshell. "I'm taking Ella back to Los Angeles with me after the funeral."

The older man gasped and reared back, stretching out a hand as though to ward him off. "*No*, Asher, no, she's all I have."

Asher's mouth tightened. *Nice.*

"That came out wrong," his father's voice hoarsened, "I didn't mean that. But you don't know what she means to me—what I mean to her—and she *knows* me."

"She knows me, too, and it's what Dee wanted."

His father shook his head and put down the drink on the end table. "No. Well, maybe when Ella was first born, before I reconnected with them...but not anymore. I *know* Ella, son, and she knows me. I'll care for her. You haven't even been around—"

"Thanks to *you*. Dee may have wanted you in her life. I don't.

"But your lifestyle...you *can't*..." He trailed off as Asher's brows shot up. "Asher." Sterling's voice was stronger now and he leaned forward and stretched out a beseeching hand. "You are not...*capable* of taking care of a five-year-old girl."

Asher got to his feet. Heat surged through him as his heart rate kicked up two notches.

"Fuck you, Sterling. I'm a helluva lot more capable than you. Dee and I had years of your brand of parenting. You think I would subject my sister's—" His voice cracked. He took a moment to gather himself and when he spoke again he had himself under control. "If you think I'd give you the opportunity to neglect another child, you are out of your goddamn mind."

"Asher, *please*. It's not just the life you live. It's the attention you draw. Do you really think it's fair to Ella to expose her to that? To the scum that follow you around, taking photos, invading your privacy—the groupies, the hangers-on? Taking her with you will invite all of that into her life and she doesn't deserve it, Asher."

Lips pressed together in an implacable line, Asher turned and strode out of the room. He paused only to grab his bag as he took the stairs two at a time to the upper level. He pushed open a door he thought he remembered led to a guest room and threw his things on the bed.

Fuck!

He hadn't even considered that. The publicity. There was no way he could allow her to be photographed and gossiped about. He paced the room. He'd just have to change things up. Dial down the lifestyle a couple of notches. Part of marketing and promoting Spade was being seen living the life. It had been years since he'd been overly enthused about the trappings. He'd just have to be careful—really careful—to shield Ella from all that. Hell, he wasn't the only celebrity to ever have a kid.

Should he go to a hotel? Nah. Ella was here and she needed to get used to him. He could survive the two days in his father's house. Barely. He'd spend time with Ella and avoid his dad.

The lawyers would work it out. He was still the legal guardian for Ella and trustee for the estate. If Dee had made changes to the will he urged her to set up when she discovered her pregnancy, he would've been notified.

So Sterling fancied himself a paragon of parenting now? Asher snorted. Screw him. Sure, Dee told him Sterling had changed. Asher was no fool. The old man was getting lonely in his old age. So what? His father had always been a selfish, manipulative bastard.

An hour later Asher had showered and lay on the bed, unable to sleep.

There was a rap at the door.

Sterling's voice came through. "Asher? The therapist is here. It's time."

Telling Ella was brutal. A dim sense of unreality set in as Asher held a confused, weeping Ella on his lap. The questions from the child came thick and fast. Questions that had no answers.

"But why can't she come back?" Ella whispered.

"I'm sorry, love. There was a car accident and her body stopped working, and she died. She can't come back," Sterling said.

Asher rubbed a hand over his eyes to disperse the moisture gathering.

"Can't we visit? I really want to see her," Ella insisted.

"Ella, she's gone, honey. She can't come back. We can't visit her. We can only remember her." Asher looked at the therapist, who gave him a nod.

Ella shook her head. "Then who is going to take care of me?"

Asher exchanged a look with his father over her head. Sterling seemed a decade older than his seventy years, his countenance ravaged by grief and sleeplessness.

"I am," Asher said. "I'm going to take good care of you, honey." He held her small, warm body close.

Ella pulled her thumb out of her mouth. "What about Grandpa?"

"I'll see you, sweetie." Sterling pressed his lips together, then lowered his head and put a hand to his brow, his shoulders shaking with silent sobs.

Asher tightened his grip.

The child twisted. "Hey, Uncle Asher."

He relaxed his arms. "Oh, sorry Ella."

The therapist spoke. "Ella, your uncle and grandpa are sad that your mommy died, too. It's okay for everyone to feel sad and cry. It doesn't feel good when someone you love dies."

After the woman left, Sterling tried to tempt Ella to eat with an assortment of cheeses, some kind of fish-shaped crackers, and sweets. No dice. His father put in an animated movie and settled Ella on his lap, where she sat with a small, ratty blanket, sucking her thumb, listless.

When it came time for Ella to go to bed, she begged his old man to lie down with her. Sterling's accusing expression met Asher's even gaze. Asher carried her little weeping body to her bedroom and laid her gently on the bed. His father took off his shoes and laid down next to the child, gathering her close.

Asher switched off the light and pulled the door behind him as he went back downstairs.

Was he doing the right thing?

He gave himself a shake. Of course he was.

• • •

A quick glance at the clock the next day indicated it was nearly noon. Asher grunted and rolled out of bed, heading for the shower. He considered his father as he studied the Moroccan tile walls of the shower, the hot water pulsing down from some fancy gadget above his head. Hard to believe a man so savvy in his business dealings could be so foolish where women were concerned.

Asher's mother Jacqueline—the scion of old Hollywood money—was beautiful and spoiled, manipulative and narcissistic. Sterling's second, brief union with a much younger woman had produced no offspring, thankfully. Delilah's mother, Katherine, was arguably the best of the lot. She was a gifted horsewoman;

unfortunately, she didn't have a nurturing bone in her body, at least not for two-legged creatures. She and Dee had a cordial relationship—and that was largely due to Dee's nature—but there was no way she would want or get custody of Ella. She may have seen her granddaughter once—twice at the most.

When Asher walked into the living room twenty minutes later, his father eyed him from the recliner, laptop open. Asher greeted Ella where she sat working on a puzzle with a kiss on the top of her head, and gave his father a nod before heading in search of coffee.

In the kitchen, an array of breakfast foods were laid out on the enormous marble island. Ignoring the food, he spied the coffee maker. Full. Good. He needed his wits about him for what was coming. He pulled out his phone. There were a number of missed text messages and voicemails. He ignored them, scrolling through until he found the one that mattered. His lawyer and the other attorney were on their way to the house.

Moments later, the doorbell rang and Sterling admitted Asher's legal team.

The discussion with the two lawyers in the study was brief. One of the men had drawn up Delilah's will when Ella was born—the terms were inarguable. Sterling was given copies of all the relevant legal documents and the men departed.

Once they had gone, Sterling pulled Asher aside. "I'll give you four months. If there are ongoing adjustment problems, if she's lonely, if you aren't parenting adequately, I'll come after you for custody."

Asher stood, motionless, his eyes narrowed to slits. "Who do you think you are? That's not for you to decide—"

His father stood his ground. "I'm her grandfather, and I love her. She knows me; she's comfortable here. Your lifestyle—"

"Here we go again. *My* lifestyle? What about yours, you son of a bitch? Dee and I only had each other growing up. You were completely MIA as a parent. Shipping us off to boarding school and then going on ski vacations while we had to do holidays with strangers?" Asher hissed.

His father met his eyes. "Yes. And I'm sorry for it. I made amends with Dee. I've handed over a lot of my responsibilities with the company. I'm not working as much—"

"Good for you," Asher spat.

"—while you work all the time, and in your business, God knows what sort of unsavory characters you have dealings with. I don't want her exposed to your lifestyle."

Asher's fists clenched. "You know *fuck all* about me and my life."

His father's demeanor was calm, his tone even. "I made mistakes with you and Dee, Asher, but I'd do anything for Ella. I owe it to her and to Dee. I'll come after you, and believe me the courts will lean in favor of a man like me over a man like you. I won't sit idly by. Four months, Asher." Sterling walked away.

Asher seethed silently, stomach roiling, and made his way back to the empty living room where he called his assistant. "Where are you?"

"Ten minutes away."

"Okay. I want out of here the day after tomorrow, first flight out after the funeral."

Justin sighed. "I thought you'd come later in the week. The jet's in Mexico, remember? That indie band—"

"Can you get it here?"

"Not that soon. Maybe Sterling—"

"Forget it. Book us first-class commercial."

"*Commercial?*"

"Just do it."

Chapter 3

Maddy's layover in Las Vegas on her way to Los Angeles was brief. So brief, she ended up running through the airport like an old-time linebacker in a rental car commercial. She was the last person on the plane before the doors closed; the flight attendant checked her seat assignment and took her to task with a cluck.

Hip joints that ached from the uncomfortable seats on the first leg of the flight were now screaming in agony after that mad dash through the airport.

Still, it was impossible to miss the movie-star handsome, vaguely familiar man and the hysterically sobbing, angelic-looking child holding onto him in a mostly empty first-class section she had to pass through to reach her own seat in row 32. The man was obviously trying to get the little girl to buckle up, but she was clinging to him like a limpet. He glared at the flight attendant, an older, gray-haired woman, who scowled back.

"Sir, we're ready to push back; she needs to be strapped in or you both need to get *off*."

Her words made the child shriek still louder—she was asking for something, but Maddy couldn't quite make it out.

Maddy put her carry-on down in the empty seat next to her and knelt next to him, wincing. She met the man's harried gaze. "What's her name?"

"Ella."

"Does she have a blanket or a toy or something?" Every child traveling needed an item of comfort. Maddy didn't have kids, but she'd been around them all her life. Stressful situations required thumbs, stuffed animals, blankets…especially at four or five, or whatever age she was.

The guy gave her a blank look. "A what?"

Why did he look so familiar?

Maddy's brow wrinkled. "A blanket?"

The child stopped crying and put her thumb in her mouth, staring at Maddy with huge, nut-brown eyes, lashes clumped together with tears.

He smiled, but it didn't reach his eyes. "Mmm…I don't know what you're talking about."

Maddy frowned. "Is this your child?"

"My niece."

Ah. That explained it. "Does she have a little blanket?"

The light dawned in those shockingly brilliant hazel eyes. "Yes," he said slowly. "Is that what she's asking for?"

Maddy nodded.

The child nodded.

"Sir," said the flight attendant.

He rose, baring his teeth in a facsimile of a grin.

The flight attendant recoiled from the look, muttering under her breath.

Maddy bit back a smile and backed up.

Opening the overhead bin, he felt around in a bag and pulled out a ratty blanket. At one time it may have been pink, but it was now a well-loved, dingy gray.

The child reached for it, expression rapt.

"You." He pointed to Maddy. "Sit there, please."

The gray-haired woman in the airline uniform shook her head. "No, sir, she has a coach seat."

He gave her that look again. "I'll pay the difference. She sits here."

The woman grumbled but nodded to Maddy to sit in the seat the man had indicated.

The man reached for her carry-on, and examined the plastic baggage tag containing her identifying information before putting it in the overhead bin. He gave the tag a tug with two fingers. "Madeline?"

That's what I get for helping. Now this guy knows my name and address. She examined him for signs that he was a creeper. What she found instead were signs of strain and sleeplessness that should have made him less attractive but didn't.

Why do I feel like I've seen this guy before? Is he an actor?

His longish hair was a rich mahogany, and he had the kind of face talent scouts dream about, chiseled perfection marred by a slightly angular, prominent nose and strong chin. By far, his most striking feature was his eyes. Hazel or brown didn't do them justice. They were golden, almost yellow in the center, edged by a dark brown ring and framed by the thickest eyelashes Maddy had ever seen.

"Please, sit," golden-eyes said.

Maddy settled into the aisle seat across the way from him.

The flight attendant picked up a phone and mumbled something into the mouthpiece about takeoff, then buckled herself into the jump seat.

Maddy snuck a look at the man again. The child had curled up against him and was starting to nod off. She was asleep before they reached cruising altitude.

After declining the flight attendant's offer for refreshment, Maddy pulled her e-reader from her bag and settled in to read in the awkward silence.

"Thank you, Madeline," he said.

"It's Maddy."

"Thanks, Maddy."

"No problem."

"As you can see, I'm a little out of my depth here." His smile was disarming as he reached out to shake her hand. "Asher Lowe."

She reached across the aisle, and he stared at her misshapen, too thin hand with its red, swollen joints.

The corners of his mouth pulled down as he took it carefully in his.

She freed her hand, and her polite smile faltered as his name registered.

Asher Lowe?

The front man for Spade? Rock god, notorious philanderer, and son of Sterling Lowe, one of the richest men in America? She searched her celebrity memory banks—they were rusty from disuse. She didn't even recognize the reality starlets who graced the covers these days, but once upon a time, she'd read entertainment magazines cover to cover. Wasn't his mom some Hollywood icon renowned for her unusual eyes? No wonder he looked familiar.

Good Lord. Was she still staring at him? His lips had quirked into an insincere half-smile. She glanced back toward coach. "Listen, everything seems to be under control here, so I can just mosey on back to my seat—"

"No." He put a hand out to stop her, his tone panicked, his body radiating tension.

The little girl sighed in her sleep and shifted against him.

"Please stay," he whispered. "Please."

"Is she nervous about flying?" Maddy asked in a low tone.

His lips twisted and he examined Maddy through narrowed eyes "Probably. It's not just that," he glanced around, "she's… Ella's…coming to live with me. Her mother was killed three days ago in a car accident."

Maddy gasped.

"We're…uh…trying to figure this out."

"*God.* I'm so sorry. How awful. Is her dad—?"

"Not around. And, as you can probably see, I don't know much about kids."

Maddy glanced at his lap where the hand not holding the child was closed into a fist, his smile belied by the tortured expression in his eyes.

"Momma?" Ella murmured in her sleep.

An expression of naked pain flashed across his face and he put his arm more securely around her.

The little girl resettled against him with a sigh.

Maddy swallowed past the lump in her throat. "If there's anything I can do…"

"Thanks."

She fingered her e-reader nervously.

"So, Maddy, do you live in Los Angeles?"

He wanted to make small talk?

"Yeah. I'm finishing a master's degree in education."

He nodded. "It's obvious you know your way around kids."

She shrugged. "My mom runs an in-home daycare and preschool. I helped out a lot growing up. How old is she?"

"Five. Kindergarten."

Maddy bit her lip, raising her eyes to meet his gaze. "Kids are amazingly resilient." She backtracked. "What I mean is…I… uh…can't imagine how she'll cope with the death of her mother, but, in general, they are adaptable. Especially at her age. It's one of the things I love about working with them."

Maddy lowered her eyes, but she could still feel his gaze, assessing her.

He grunted. "You from L.A.?"

"No, a little town in Virginia, about an hour from DC."

"I thought I heard the trace of a southern accent."

She laughed, softly. "And here I thought I'd beaten it back."

"So why Los Angeles?"

She met his eyes. Kind of a personal question, but he had certainly shared a doozy with her. Then again, maybe it was common knowledge? People like the Lowes were fodder for the news magazines. "Lots of reasons. I wanted a change from the East Coast…the winters can be tough."

His gaze dropped to her lap, then moved back to her face. "I couldn't help noticing…"

"It's rheumatoid arthritis," she said, steeling herself for the "helpful" suggestions that usually followed that revelation. Starting with "Aren't you a little—"

He cocked his head. "Arthritis? Aren't you a little young?"

With an inward sigh she launched into her twenty second spiel. "Not osteoarthritis. Rheumatoid. Different thing altogether. RA is an autoimmune disorder. You can have it show up as a child or adult." If she had a dollar for every time she explained this to someone, she wouldn't have any outstanding student loans.

"And yours?"

"I was diagnosed as a teenager."

"Tough," he said, his expression sympathetic.

She shrugged. "I don't let it hold me back."

"Looks painful."

She didn't respond, rubbing her fingers self-consciously. Desperate to change the subject, she blurted the first thing that came to mind. "Were you close with your sister?" She regretted the question as soon as it was out of her mouth. The expression of grief that crossed his face made her wince. "I'm sorry. I shouldn't have asked."

He rubbed a hand over his eyes. "No, it's okay. Yeah, we were close. She's my only sister—we had the same dad, different mothers, but it wasn't…we were close." The flight attendant saved

Maddy from sticking her foot in her mouth again by starting the snack service, and Ella awoke. She stared at the cold sandwich with disinterest.

"Ella, please eat," he urged.

"But I don't like it."

Maddy reached into the a la carte menu in the seat pocket in front of her. She flipped it open and pointed to an item. She noticed he couldn't seem to tear his eyes away from her hands. When he finally raised his eyes to scrutinize her, she had schooled her features into neutrality. She was used to people staring.

He looked at Maddy in askance and made a face at the items she indicated. "Applesauce and goldfish?"

Ella lit up. "Oh yes, Uncle Asher. I'm hungry."

He mouthed "thank you" to Maddy and pushed the bell for the flight attendant.

• • •

For the remainder of the flight, Asher sat back as Ella and Maddy discussed kindergarten, fairies, and favorite movies across him. It was like listening to a foreign language. Ella was animated for the first time since they had broken the news to her, and she'd gone an hour without sobbing. Maddy had a real knack for drawing her out. Progress.

The woman was attractive—pretty, really. Her thick, brown hair framed an oval face with high cheekbones. Her complexion was skin care–commercial beautiful, and her eyes—not quite blue, closer to the gray of the Pacific Ocean on a foggy day—were serious under delicately winged brows. She was thin, too thin to his mind, and he was accustomed to thin women, living in Los Angeles. Was her weight related to her disease?

She was good with Ella.

He glanced at her ring finger. Bare. Not that a ringless finger meant anything. He'd have someone check into her background. His assistant was vetting some of the best nannies in the business, but this Madeline Anderson had made Ella smile for the first time in days, had plenty of experience working with kids, and seemed unfazed by the Lowe name. It wouldn't hurt to have her investigated, just in case.

Chapter 4

Maddy popped a bagel in the toaster and poured herself a glass of orange juice. Leisurely breakfasts were a rarity these days. Her course load was light in her final semester with no student teaching, but there was always overtime at the coffee shop, and morning shifts there were insane. Maybe she'd bring a book and blanket and enjoy a lazy Sunday at the park a few blocks away.

Her cell phone rang and she glanced at the screen. A local Los Angeles exchange but not a number she recognized. Her eyes narrowed. *Please don't let it be work.* She couldn't say no to extra shifts, but it was shaping up to be a beautiful day outside. Maybe she should let it go to voicemail? No, she really could use the money. Sighing, she took the call.

"Hello?"

"Maddy?" said a deep voice on the other end of the phone.

A chill went up her spine. It had been two weeks, but she knew that voice. She ought to by now. She'd had a continuous loop of Spade in rotation on her iPod since her encounter with Asher Lowe on the plane.

"Mr. Lowe?"

"Yeah. Call me Asher."

"How are you guys? I've been wondering how Ella's adjusting." How *does* a five-year old cope with losing her only parent and getting him for a guardian? He'd seemed ill-equipped on the plane.

He cleared his throat. "Not good."

"I'm sorry."

"Listen, will you come to my house?" he asked. "I can have a car bring you."

Maddy frowned. "Uh…why?"

"I wanted to talk to you about Ella."

"Oh, I guess. I…I have a car. If you give me your address I can—"

"The car's ready when you are."

"Excuse me?"

"The car's waiting." She peered out the window of her apartment. Sure enough, there was a black town car at the curb. She frowned. How the hell did he know where she lived? She remembered him looking at the tag on her luggage. He must have a good memory. Still, he sent a car before she agreed to meet with him? Cocky. Or desperate. Probably both. "Oh, okay…but—"

"See you in a bit." He disconnected the call.

• • •

Maddy looked out the window as the driver pulled into a gated driveway in a very exclusive part of Santa Monica. Once buzzed in, the gates opened, allowing the sleek car to make its way up the drive. Her eyes widened.

Now *that* was a big house. At the top of the driveway loomed an enormous, white stucco, red-tiled, Tuscan style building. Red and pink bougainvillea wound their way nearly two stories up on trellises lining the front walls on either side of massive front doors. She'd never had occasion to be in this part of Los Angeles. Probably because she'd never done one of those star tours of celebrity homes in the open-air mini-buses like the one their car had just passed. It was filled with tourists and their cameras, leaning out the windows, eager for a glimpse of a celebrity. Even a celebrity's dog would do.

The car came to a smooth halt at the apex of the circular driveway.

"Thank you," she said to the driver when he put the car in park. He nodded over his shoulder.

"No problem, Miss." Exiting the vehicle, he came around to open her door.

Maddy climbed the front steps and rang the bell. The door was opened by a tall, lean, dark-haired man with brown eyes and a warm smile. He was casually dressed in jeans and the kind of classic T-shirt that was either vintage or top-dollar designer.

"Hi." She reached to shake his hand. "I'm Maddy. Asher called me."

"Hey, Maddy, we've been expecting you. C'mon in."

She stepped over the threshold and he closed the door behind her.

"I'm Justin Montoya, Asher's personal assistant."

Maddy glanced around. This place was a freakin' palace but tastefully decorated. Nothing *Cribs*-like to mock here, though it was easily the largest house she'd ever been in—not counting the White House tour she'd taken in college.

"Why don't you come with me?"

She followed him down the long hallway to the rear of the house, and they entered a study with views of a pool in the middle of a flowering garden. Maddy wandered over to the French doors that led to a patio.

"Asher will be in shortly. Can I get you anything?"

Maddy clasped her hands together. "No, thanks. Um…how's Ella?"

Justin shook his head. "Not good, Maddy. We don't know what we're doing," he said, spreading out his hands. "We're all out of our element here, and poor Ella is having a rough time."

The door opened and Asher strode in. Her lungs seized up. Dressed casually in a form-fitting T-shirt and worn Levi's that lovingly followed every hard line of his body, it was impossible not to notice his masculinity or his fatigue. Dark circles bruised the underside of his golden eyes.

"Thanks, Justin," Asher said.

"Need anything?" the assistant asked on his way out.

Asher turned to Maddy, brows raised.

She shook her head.

"We're good, thanks," Asher said.

Justin left the room, quietly shutting the study door.

Asher gave Maddy another one of those smiles that didn't reach his eyes. "Have a seat, please." He gestured toward the sofa.

She sat on the edge of the sectional and studied him. By the looks of him, he wasn't getting much sleep. Was that part and parcel for a rock star, or were things with Ella that difficult? In the weeks since she'd met him on the plane, she was ashamed to admit she'd read everything there was to know about him and Spade. And none of it made her hopeful about his chances of successfully parenting a five-year-old girl—not the way he lived with touring, partying, and player-ing.

"I need help with Ella."

Of course he did. If he hadn't hung up on her so abruptly, she could've saved them both time and inconvenience. "Oh. Well, I'd be happy to help out occasionally with some babysitting—"

"No, I need a full-time nanny."

"I'm sorry. I could've saved you the time and car and driver. I'm in school—"

"I know. But you also work full-time in a coffee house, right?"

Her brows knitted together. "Uh…yeah." How did he even know that?

"We can accommodate your class schedule."

"I'm sorry?"

"You can finish your degree. This is your last semester, right?"

She must have mentioned it on the plane, but the thing was, she didn't remember telling him that.

"I'm not a nanny."

"I know. But you have the relevant experience. And I'll pay you more than you make serving up cappuccinos."

"It's not that simple." She worked as a barista because the chain extended health benefits to their employees. Nannies didn't get benefits. She couldn't afford to be without coverage, and it would be expensive to buy her own health insurance. Even if they would accept her, which was doubtful, the coverage would be abysmal. When something happened with her rheumatoid arthritis, she'd suffocate in debt trying to cover medical bills. The school loans were bad enough.

"Sure it is." He raked a hand through artfully mussed hair. He probably paid a fortune to have it look like that, she thought uncharitably.

"Have you tried to find someone?" There was no doubt someone with his affluence could get the best nanny in Los Angeles.

He prowled the room. "Yeah, but I haven't found a good fit."

She frowned. "I find that hard to believe."

"I've been trying for almost two weeks. I've had the best people on this. We've interviewed two dozen women and one highly recommended *manny,* and it just doesn't work." His control slipped a bit on the last word as his voice rose. "She's seeing a therapist and I've been in constant contact with the woman so I know what to expect, but…"

"But?"

"I can't handle it!" he half-shouted, pacing in front of her. "She still doesn't get it!" His mouth twisted. "She cries. Weeps. Says her stomach hurts. Doesn't want to go to school. She's afraid of the dark and comes in my room at all hours." He ran hands through his hair again. It no longer appeared so artful. "She wants to sleep in my bed—when she's willing to sleep at all."

Maddy's heart lurched.

His voice shook when he said, "She wants to know if her mommy will come back if she's good. *Jesus*."

Her eyes burned and she blinked rapidly. *That poor kid.* Asher was stirring up no small measure of sympathy too.

He threw himself down onto the couch next to her, and Maddy surveyed his red-rimmed eyes. "Asher, I think…I mean…isn't that the normal response to what she's going through?"

"Yeah. Or so the therapist says."

"It's going to take time for her to understand."

He groaned.

"You need to stay calm, loving, and patient. I'm sure you're doing fine."

Asher raised his brows. "Maddy, I'm a lot of things, but patient doesn't make the list." He leaned back against the couch and stared at the ceiling.

She'd worked a lot with kids that age, since her emphasis was in elementary education and she'd grown up with hordes of preschoolers, but this was far outside her experience. She'd lost her father, but that was different; she'd never even had a chance to know him.

"All I can tell you is you're dealing with someone who believes in fairies, Santa Claus, and unicorns. In wishes coming true—in magic. Of *course* she believes her mother is coming back." She waited until he met her gaze. When he did, his eyes were haunted. "Asher, you can't help her until you help yourself. How are you dealing with your grief?"

He scowled. "I'm not the problem."

"Do you have someone to talk to about the loss of your sister? Maybe if you—"

"Not going to happen."

"I mean a friend, Asher, not necessarily a therapist."

He grunted.

She inched farther back on the couch. "I have to complete my degree this semester."

"I already told you that wouldn't be a problem," he stated.

She looked up at the ceiling. "I…you don't know anything about me."

"I know enough. And I'm a good judge of people. Ella warmed up to you on the plane. You checked out. You're a bit over-qualified, but I think we can come to an agreement on salary."

She bit her lip. "It's not so much the salary. I'd like to help you guys, but—"

"The health insurance? No problem. I can provide excellent health benefits."

Her eyes narrowed. It was weird and more than a little disturbing how much he knew about her. Granted, she'd admitted she had an autoimmune disease on the plane, but he was picking up on all kinds of subtleties. She met his glance and saw what she hadn't paid attention to in her previous encounter with him: keen intelligence in the depths of those absurdly glamorous eyes.

He leaned toward her and stretched out a hand, beseeching. "Do this for me then. Interview a couple of prospective nannies. Find me someone we both agree on this week or take the job. I'm desperate, Maddy."

His expression was pleading but his eyes were cold. She couldn't shake the feeling she was being manipulated. This town was full of nannies. Hell, he had the funds to import one. He could find the reincarnation of Mary Poppins, if he wanted.

"I'd be happy to help find you someone qualified."

"Do we have an agreement? If you fail, you take the job."

How hard could it be?

Chapter 5

When Maddy arrived at Asher's home the next morning, Ella met her at the door, peeking out from behind Justin.

"Hi, Ella. Do you remember me from the plane?"

Ella nodded, thumb tucked firmly between her lips, her somber milk chocolate–colored eyes giving Maddy the once-over. Maddy walked over to the marble staircase and sat on the second-to-last step. She patted the space next to her and Ella wandered over.

"Maddy, I'm heading out to the patio, okay? I need to walk Ella to the bus stop in fifteen minutes," Justin said.

"Can I take you, Ella?" Maddy asked.

The child studied her, expression serious, then nodded.

"Justin, she'll direct me to the bus stop, and I'll come back and help."

"Great. Can I get you coffee? Tea?" he asked.

"No, I'm good."

Justin disappeared and Maddy turned to Ella.

"How're you doing?"

The little girl shrugged.

"You miss your mom?"

"Uh huh."

Maddy put her arm around the child and gave her a squeeze. "I understand. My daddy died when I was little. I missed him a lot."

"Your daddy died?"

"Yep. But my mom told me I could talk to him anytime I wanted, and he'd always be listening and watching out for me."

"He *is*?"

"Yes. The same way your mom is listening and watching over you."

Ella leaned back to stare at Maddy. "*Is* she?" she breathed, looking around the foyer.

43

"She is," Maddy whispered. "And she's sending all her love to you, too."

"*All* of it? How come Uncle Asher and Grandpa didn't tell me?" she whispered back, scandalized.

"Hmmm. I don't know."

The child considered her, suspicion warring with hope. "Can she talk to me?"

Maddy shook her head. "No. My dad wasn't able to talk to me either. But even though he didn't talk to me and he couldn't ever come back, I know he listens when I talk to him."

The child nodded wide-eyed and settled against her. "Are you going to take care of me?"

Maddy's heart flipped over. "Your Uncle Asher takes care of you, sweetie."

"Can *you* stay with me?"

"I'll be here for a bit. Should we get your things together to walk to the bus?"

Ella nodded and put her little hand in Maddy's.

• • •

Justin was a gem, a master of efficiency with a quick mind who was receiving updates from the three most reputable nanny agencies in LA.

"So, this has to be a live-in position?" she asked.

"Definitely."

"Why?"

Justin gave her a look, brows arched over the tops of his sunglasses. They were sitting in the shade by the pool, laptops on the patio table. "You do know what he does, right? The rock thing?"

"Yeah. So, odd hours?"

"Yep."

"Why don't you? Seems like plenty of room."

"I have. When I was between boyfriends." He shrugged. "But I've been living with Scott for a few years now and we have a home together."

"Oh, I didn't know you were serious about someone. That makes sense."

"Besides, much as I love Asher," he glanced from the computer screen to her, "love him like a brother, not an employer, I don't want the job to consume my life. I'll help as much as I can, but I don't know anything about kids, Maddy. I'm as useless as Asher."

Maddy laughed. "Not so useless. Ella likes you."

He flashed her a grin, exposing absurdly perfect teeth. "She's a great kid." The smile vanished. "Listen, I don't talk about Asher with people 'cause he likes his privacy, you know? He has that rock star persona you've probably seen by now—the charm, the arrogance. But underneath all of the shtick there's a great guy. A wicked-smart, loyal guy. The thing is…" Justin shifted in his chair.

Maddy cocked her head. "What?"

He sighed. "You seem like a down-to-earth person, but Asher can be very…engaging."

Maddy leaned back and crossed her arms over her chest. "Believe me, Justin, you don't need to warn me about the Asher Lowes of the world."

"Yeah, well, I don't care if you're a man or woman, straight or gay, when Asher Lowe turns on the charm, it's compelling."

Maddy gave a short laugh. "Not interested. You don't need to warn me away from a forty-year-old playboy rock star born with a silver spoon in his mouth."

Justin said, "But that's just it, Maddy, he's a lot more than that."

"Whatever. Not interested." She resumed her search of job applicants.

Maddy hadn't had particularly good luck with relationships, and Asher Lowe was more like a different species than a man. Between work and school, she didn't have time for much of a dating life. Two casual relationships shortly after landing on the West Coast was all she'd managed. The only lasting relationship she'd had was with Trey, her college boyfriend. They'd been inseparable for most of two years. Hell, she'd loved him, but after what happened, she'd learned to be more careful with her heart. There had been a series of guys since college, but the relationships were strictly for fun. They ran their course and ended painlessly.

By noon, they had identified four good candidates and went about setting up interviews.

"Asher insists on meeting them."

"Fine. After we've vetted them, he can meet them."

Justin shook his head. "Nope. He won't go for that, but he did say he'd make himself available."

"You said earlier he's rarely up before noon, and out of the house most of the day."

Justin let out a sigh. "Let's set them up back to back starting at eleven thirty. I'll make sure he's available."

• • •

At eleven thirty the next morning, the first candidate arrived. She was an athletic blonde in yoga pants, the outline of a red running bra visible through her yellow flowered top. Attractive and vivacious, she had a degree in early childhood development and rave recommendations from previous employers. Maddy smiled at Justin. This girl would make an excellent nanny. Maddy seated her on the far side of the room with some paperwork.

She sidled up to Justin. "Perfect, right? This one just oozes spunk."

He gave her funny look. A moment later, Asher strode into the living room, clad in snug, faded Levi's, and a tight, sleeveless Guns N' Roses cutoff T-shirt that revealed tattooed biceps. Sunglasses and black combat boots completed the outfit.

It was all Maddy could do not to gawk. He looked rested and… hot. The quintessential rock god in that getup.

Asher crossed the room, gave the girl a wicked half-grin, and took her hand in both of his. He drew her in, leaning close—too close—in a clear invasion of the girl's personal space. But she didn't draw away. Instead, she leaned in and her nostrils flared as she stared wide-eyed, cheeks a mottled red.

Good God. Was she…was the girl *sniffing* him? Maddy recoiled.

"Hi, Krista, Asher Lowe," he rumbled.

Maddy perched on the edge of the ottoman, frozen with horror as Asher poured charm like syrup all over her; the girl was completely star-struck. A quick glance at Justin showed he was having difficulty keeping a straight face.

Within fifteen minutes, Asher was escorting the girl from the room, and he was on the receiving end of a litany of her favorite Spade songs and live shows.

Asher glared over his shoulder at Maddy.

Maddy leaned back, mouth agape.

Justin couldn't hold back his laughter.

"That was disgusting," she said.

Justin rubbed a hand over his face. "I'll admit that was particularly bad. Are you starting to get some inkling of why this is so hard?"

"Is that what it's been like?"

"Pretty much. I tried to warn you."

"I don't get it, she seemed like a reasonable person. I mean, he's not all *that*."

"Apparently he is…to some. Thankfully, not to you."

"Is it the charm or the celebrity or the money? What?"

"Dunno. But we've had a number of interviews end that way." Maddy pretended to shudder.

"What about an older woman?" she asked.

"We've interviewed one, but Asher thinks it should be someone young and energetic like Ella's mom."

"Men?"

"There aren't as many. We figured with so many men in Ella's life, she could benefit from being around a woman, and the therapist agreed."

Maddy pulled out her list. "Married women?"

"Unlikely to want to live in."

"Right. A lesbian?" she joked.

"I don't think that should be asked in the employment process," Justin said seriously.

"No, you're right, I was…never mind."

"Maddy, you seem immune. You should take the job."

She made a face.

Asher strode back in and slammed the door, his jaw set, sunglasses no longer in evidence.

Maddy raised her eyebrows at Justin. *Yeah. Charm personified.* Asher turned to Maddy and opened his mouth to speak.

She held up a hand. "Okay, okay," she said. "I begin to see the magnitude of the problem. Give us another chance. We have a couple of potentials—"

"Just so you understand, I want someone who is one-hundred-

and-twenty percent about Ella. I don't want someone who gives," Asher snapped his fingers, "*that* for me."

By the end of the week, Maddy was forced to admit it was hopeless. People—young women in L.A. at least—had such a *thing* about celebrity in general and Asher Lowe in particular. There were a few reasonable candidates, women who didn't get sucked into the whirlpool of his attentions. In fact, a couple of women were downright disdainful. But by mid-week, Maddy was finding flaws in most of those candidates as well. Ridiculous flaws. Flaws that made Justin grin. The real trouble was, after spending most of the week at the house, walking Ella to and from the bus stop and hanging out with the child before leaving each day, Maddy was coming to the uncomfortable conclusion that she was falling in love.

With Ella.

She wanted to care for Ella. And she was growing more concerned about Asher's ability and willingness to be a true guardian to the child by the day. He hadn't adapted his schedule to hers, and he was hopeless as a disciplinarian. She was no expert, but after years of helping her mom with the daycare, not to mention all the student teaching, she had an understanding of the basics: sleep, food, and discipline.

It was increasingly obvious that Asher didn't want to discipline Maddy about anything because he pitied her.

On Friday, she told Justin she would take the job.

"That's awesome, Maddy. I'll get the employment contract together. There's the usual stuff and then there's the celebrity specific stuff—you'll have to sign a confidentiality agreement. Asher has already taken care of the background—"

"Excuse me?"

He shifted in his chair and couldn't meet her eyes. "Oh, I'm sorry, I spoke out of turn. Never mind."

Maddy stared at Justin, who was looking anywhere but at her. "My God. He had me *investigated?*"

"Maddy, it's standard in this business. Granted, it usually happens after an offer is extended, but Asher had a feeling about you from the first time you met."

"He hired someone to check into my background?"

"Well, yeah. Honestly Maddy, the Lowes can't be too careful. You know who Asher's father is, and Spade, well…"

It felt wrong. Really wrong. "Is that even legal?"

"Well, yeah, I'm assuming he just ran a standard background check. You'd be surprised how much information is out there, if you have the right person—" He caught sight of the expression on her face.

Her stomach churned. *What a violation.* What did he know about her and her life? The abysmal state of her finances? Hospitalizations? Drunken table-dancing in Mazatlan years ago during spring break? *Her sex life?*

"Listen, Maddy, they all do it—at this level. This is the world they live in," he shrugged, "and it's a weird one. Especially for someone from a small town. Hell, I'm from a small town. I remember how shocked I was when I first started out in this business working with these people. But you have to understand, with the kind of money Asher has, add in his father's fortune… well, there are lots of shady characters out there. And this is his niece we're talking about. The child of the person he loved most in the world. He can't be too careful."

Maddy pressed her lips together but finally nodded.

"So you have health insurance currently, right?"

"Yeah, that's why I have to work full-time as a barista and only go to grad school part-time."

"Is it painful? It looks painful," he said, staring at a spot just above her swollen hands.

"Sometimes." *All the time.* "But it doesn't hold me back."

• • •

A week later, Maddy sat on a barstool in Asher's kitchen finishing her cereal with raspberries. Fresh raspberries. What a luxury. It wasn't even raspberry season—at least in this part of the world. Rinsing her dish, she placed it in the dishwasher and headed into the hallway. The phone in her pocket rang and she plucked it out. Confused, she stared at the face. A blocked number.

She answered cautiously. "Hello?"

"Madeline Anderson?"

"Speaking."

"This is Sterling Lowe."

Maddy froze.

"I'm Ella's grandfather."

"Yeah, I know who you are."

"Good. I have some things to discuss with you."

Maddy knew a bad situation when it came calling. Justin had explained the custody issue. Talking to Sterling Lowe could only get her into trouble. "I don't think—"

"Don't think, listen."

Maddy's frown deepened into a scowl. *Asshole.*

"I'm sure Asher has explained the situation with the custody?"

Maddy mentally counted to ten to remove the temptation to speak. The man grunted. "I want you to help me get custody."

Her stomach churned. "I don't want to be in the middle of this. I'm just the hired help—"

"I understand," he said, apparently taking a new tack; his tone became soothing. "But Asher is not a good guardian for my granddaughter. I'm sure you can see that already."

Anger burned, mixing with the cold, hard knot in the pit of her stomach.

"Well, no, Mr. Lowe, I don't see that. I've only been here a few days. I'm here to help Asher figure stuff out with Ella, and he pays me a good wage. If you have issues, you take them up with him."

"Well m'dear, if I could do that I wouldn't need you. I want what's best for Ella. And if you don't now, you will."

"Mr. Lowe, I refuse to be dragged—"

The man's tone hardened. "Tough. You are. If you help me, I'll pay you well."

Maddy clenched her fist. "No. Goodbye, Mr. Lowe."

"I'll foreclose on your mother's house."

What?

The pit at the bottom of her stomach swallowed her up, and her jaw dropped. "What did you say?" she whispered.

"Your mother. She's been unable to refinance—something about a bankruptcy in the past."

Maddy stopped pacing and dropped onto the couch cushion.

My God. Bankruptcy?

She knew her mom had struggled to pay years of Maddy's medical bills, but bankruptcy?

The silence lengthened.

He made a tsking sound. "You didn't know? She's been getting further and further behind since she wasn't able to qualify for a good rate. Something about a home equity loan for improvements years ago. And her credit score is abysmal. Bankruptcy tends to do that."

"She's…she's going to lose the house?"

"The house, her livelihood. I understand she runs a childcare in her home?"

Maddy stared into space, her eyes filling with tears.

He made another sound into the phone. In someone less ruthless, it might have been pity.

"The bank can take the house any day."

"What…what can I do?"

"Have you got twenty-three thousand dollars?"

She put a hand to her throat. "No," she said, almost inaudibly.

"Not a problem. I'll prevent the foreclosure—hell, I'll pay off the house."

Maddy put a trembling hand to her eyes. This was her fault. And now her mom was going to lose her income. In that tiny town where there were hardly any jobs. "I…I…can't…"

He sighed. "Here's the thing, Maddy. I want what's best for Ella. Period. Not what's best for me. Not what's best for Asher. I don't like threatening you like this, I really don't. Even for me, it's a bit heavy-handed. But I need to know Ella is getting the best care, the most love and attention possible. She'd get that from me. She won't get it from Asher, trust me."

A sob escaped her. She covered her mouth with her hand.

"He's not a bad guy." His tone was soothing. "But he's not equipped for this. He's at the wrong stage in life to do what it takes to raise a five-year-old child, even if he wanted to. I'm not asking you to do anything immoral. You won't need to make stuff up. Just keep records of what makes him unfit and testify to that when the time comes."

Maddy gritted her teeth, holding in another sob.

His voice hardened. "Do we have a deal?"

Twenty-three thousand dollars? Her mom with no home, no way to run the daycare? Asher was paying her well, but if the foreclosure was imminent…

"But what if he's capable? What if he *is* fit?" But he wasn't, not by a long shot. Maddy had been living here a week, and

Asher exhibited little interest in Ella. Asher's ambivalence was so disturbing, she'd planned to speak to the child's therapist about it.

Sterling Lowe's noise this time sounded like a snort. "He isn't. The apple didn't fall far from that tree," he stated, cryptically.

"I'll need to call my mom, to verify—"

"I've e-mailed you a letter from the bank to your mom detailing what she owes. Put me on hold and see."

Maddy pulled out her laptop and logged in. There was one e-mail in her inbox. She opened it and the attachment.

There it was in black and white. Twenty-three thousand, four hundred fifteen dollars and eighty-one cents. A third and final notice of foreclosure from her mother's bank.

"What if they foreclose before…"

"I won't let that happen. And I'll relieve your mom's mind by having them send a letter stating they've extended the time frame. She's tried a number of things to prevent the foreclosure—partial payments and the like—but she's too far in arrears."

"Can you stop it?"

There was a humorless laugh from the other end. "I thought you said you knew who I was?"

She wiped at tears trailing down her cheeks. She didn't know anyone who could loan her that kind of cash. Maybe if she told Asher? She discarded the idea immediately. He would most likely fire her on the spot if she admitted Sterling Lowe had contacted her. She could refuse and go get another full-time job. But one that would pay twenty thousand in a short period of time? No. Her dancing hadn't improved that much since her college days.

Then there was the not-so-simple matter of her health insurance. She'd quit the coffee shop, and even if they did hire her back, there would be a wait because of her pre-existing condition.

"Maddy, I'm waiting for your answer."

Bile gathered at the back of her throat. "I'll think about it." At least that would buy her time.

"You'll see, Maddy. He's not capable, and despite what you must think of me after this phone call," he cleared his throat, "I love Ella and I'd do anything for her." He hung up.

Maddy glared at the cell phone in her lap. What a family. Asher wanted custody but didn't want to parent. But his dad? She shuddered. How could *that* be good for Ella? Talk about the lesser of two evils. Maybe she could turn Asher into a better parent? He'd have to want it. She worried her bottom lip between her teeth. Once she had regained some semblance of control, she picked up the phone and dialed her mother.

"Maddy, sweetheart, it's good to hear your voice." Her tone sharpened with worry. "Is everything all right?"

"Yeah." She sniffed and coughed to cover it.

"Are you sick?" There was real concern in her mom's voice now.

"No, no. I'm good. What about *you,* Mom?"

Her mother let out a weary sigh. "I'm okay, Maddylove. Things are tough, but I'll manage, I always do."

"Tough? How?"

"Nothing for you to worry about. The twins moved away, so I have fewer students. I've got more improvements to make to the house to be up to code but, well, never mind. How's the new job?"

Maddy stared up at the ceiling and blinked rapidly. 'Sokay, the little girl is sweet."

"Poor thing."

"I know."

"If you need me, call or e-mail—you know e-mail works better with the time difference, hon. I don't have any part-time help right now, so it's tough to talk during the week. You know, I've some experience with kids dealing with grief."

"Me and Dad?"

"Well, yeah. But we also had the Flemmings' son. He was four when his mother died, remember? They had his therapist come talk to me about stuff to watch for."

"Oh, yeah. That was really sad. Aneurism, right?"

"Yep. Listen, sugar, I gotta get these kids some lunch. Talk to you later?"

"Okay. Love you."

"You too."

Maddy buried her face in her hands and wept.

• • •

Asher walked up the steps to the house and let himself in. It had been the worst kind of day, an entire day spent in meetings, but the discrepancies with one of Spade's accounts could not be ignored. He'd be hiring another forensic accountant and firing a manager shortly. He was one to wrap his fingers tightly around the pulse of the empire that was Spade. It wasn't that he didn't have the best band manager in the business, the best accountant, financial manager and right on down the line. It was that he'd learned from his father that placing too much trust in other people to manage vast sums of money—and people—was ill advised.

Then there were the creative differences he routinely had with some of the band members. They went through this periodically. Spade was commercially successful. Critically? Not so much. Every once in a while, someone in the band would get a wild hair to try something new, a radical departure from their trademark sound. He and the rest of the band might concede a song on an album or something played at a show. But Spade was successful year after year for hewing to the tried and true. They had lost plenty of great musicians over creative differences over the last two decades.

And why couldn't he follow through on the interest from the blonde model-actress with the wide smile at the record release party? She'd rubbed herself all over him and was just what he needed: no strings, stress relief in a hotel room. But something wasn't right, and he couldn't seem to get an erection to save his goddamn life.

Since Dee's death, he'd had trouble mustering enthusiasm for much. It was baffling, this emotional numbness and depleted libido. Of course Dee's death impacted him. But why was it fucking with his sex life? That was just plain wrong.

Maddy put Ella to bed at the ridiculously early hour of eight P.M. so, as usual, he wouldn't get a chance to see his niece today. Weekdays she was in school before he woke up and in bed before he got home. Maddy needed to relax on the bedtime. Kids didn't need that much sleep. He'd like to see Ella, spend some time with her, maybe take her out to dinner.

All the lights were off in the foyer, but he could hear the murmur of voices from the rear of the house. Asher took two steps forward, barely able to see as his eyes tried to adjust from the glare of the outside motion-detecting spotlight, and straight into something solid in the hallway. He crashed to his knees.

"*Damn it*. What the—"

A light came on. He pushed himself back to a standing position, staring in confusion at the proliferation of boxes in the hallway. There must have been twenty odd boxes stacked up. Maddy appeared, noiselessly, from the rear of the house. She walked up to him, head cocked. "You okay?" she asked.

"Yeah. What's all this? Your stuff?"

She tilted her head. "*My* stuff? No, Asher, this is Delilah's stuff."

He stood, paralyzed in his effort to tamp down the upwelling of grief. "What's it doing here?" he finally asked, gruffly. She shrugged. "Beats me. It arrived this afternoon."

Asher approached the boxes, a cold, hard knot of dread in his abdomen. There was no way he would go through her things. He was still trying to pretend she was alive. "They need to go to the garage in the morning."

Maddy's lips twisted. "You want me to move them to the garage?"

He shook his head, unable to stop himself from glancing at her hands. "No, of course not. Have someone do it."

Her eyes narrowed. "You think I can't move some boxes?"

"Quit being so sensitive. There are upwards of twenty boxes here and I have no idea how heavy they are. And that's not your job. Talk to Justin. There must be someone—a grounds person—who can manage it."

She looked somewhat mollified. "I'll ask when I see him in the morning." Maddy studied him in the pause that followed. "Asher, some of the things in there might be Ella's. Things she wants, stuff that reminds her of home or her mom."

Asher took an involuntary step away from the boxes.

"Maybe you should go through—"

The grief came up again and his throat tightened. He put up his hands. "No. I'm not doing that. You and Justin open it, and if it's Ella's stuff, make it fit. If it's Dee's stuff…just…just have it stacked in one of the guest rooms."

"Asher, you all right?"

He ran a hand over his face. "Yeah, yeah. Tired, long day."

She took a step closer and peered up into his face. She was still in the shadows, but he could see her thick, dark hair was down, shaping her slightly exotic features. Her wide gray eyes had something in their depths—pity? He glanced down her body. What on earth was she wearing? "What are those things on your pajamas?"

She took two steps back and crossed her arms. But it was too late.

He took a step closer and squinted. "Unicorns and rainbows?"

Her eyes narrowed to slits. "Ella loves them."

"I'll bet she does."

They were so long they covered the tops of her feet, and Maddy was practically swimming in them. He gave a short laugh. That was Maddy all right. If he'd hired one of the other nannies, she'd probably be standing here in a negligee.

He gave her his best leer. "Want to come and have some hot cocoa with me, little girl?"

Maddy flashed him a genuine grin. "Sure." She followed Asher into the kitchen. "Plain hot chocolate, right?"

"No spiking. No lacing. "

Her grin widened.

He poured water into two mugs, pulled down three tins, and laid them on the counter. "We have mint, spicy or regular."

She examined the tins. "Fancy."

"I'm a chocolate fan, it's one of my many vices." He shrugged.

"That I can believe. I'll try mint."

Putting the mugs in the microwave and setting it, he turned to her. "So how's it been going?" His gaze drifted down. An adult woman in cotton unicorn pajamas in his kitchen. That was a first.

She pulled her hair back with one hand. The movement pulled the too-big flannel top across her chest and he got a glimpse of one perfectly shaped breast where the top gaped between buttons.

A surge of lust went through him.

He blinked.

Hello.

"Asher?"

He gave his head a shake. What the hell was that? He couldn't get enthused about the model with perfect tits, but got hard with a glimpse of side-boob? He shuddered. "Yeah?" Turning back to the microwave, he concentrated on the two spinning mugs.

"We need to talk about Ella."

"Okay." He glanced over his shoulder and nodded for her to sit on the barstool at the kitchen island. "I'll bring these over."

The microwave dinged as she settled herself on the stool.

He opened the mint tin and put two spoonfuls into her mug, stirred, closed it, then did the same with the spicy hot chocolate.

Carrying the steaming mugs over, he put them down.

"Shot of milk?" he asked over his shoulder, moving toward the fridge.

She grinned, showing a row of even white teeth. "Shot of milk sounds good."

His brain conjured an image of her laid out on his kitchen island, the ridiculous pajama top pushed up, while he licked milk out of the smooth divot of her belly button. Semi-aroused, he went to one-fifty in a millisecond. He moved a hand to adjust his suddenly uncomfortable jeans.

What the fuck?

Sticking to his offer, he opened the refrigerator, took out the milk and carried it over. He poured it into their mugs and put it away.

When he came back to the island, she was blowing on her mug. *God. Her lips.* How had he never noticed them before? Full and perfect, her lower lip was slightly smaller than her upper. Now the inappropriate fantasies were raging.

Get a grip. She's the fucking nanny.

He settled onto the stool next to her, forced a smile and took a gulp of hot chocolate.

She turned to face him. He didn't dare look down to her legs, where her feet were propped on the rungs. God knows what his libido, suddenly in overdrive, would do with that image. Probably imagine her firm calves wrapped around his neck, while he—

"I know I haven't been here long but…" She rubbed her lips together.

Was she being deliberately provoking? His brows drew together as he met her eyes. Nope. They were full of innocent concern. It wasn't her. Something was wrong with him.

Celibacy.

He'd probably get worked up over any female after four weeks of abstinence. Whatever had been going on with his psyche the last few weeks was fixed. He let out a sigh of relief. It wasn't her.

"Asher?"

"Yeah, I'm listening," he said, returning his focus to the hot chocolate.

She sighed heavily. "I really want this to work out."

He raised his eyebrows and contemplated her. "Isn't it?"

Her even, white teeth toyed with her lower lip again. He almost groaned aloud; his libido was back with a vengeance.

"Let me put it another way. You and Ella need to bond."

He frowned. "Aren't we?"

"Uh…no."

Confusion warred with impatience. "You've only been here a few days."

"More than a week actually, but you're hardly around. I think you need to start as you mean to go on."

Sounded like lyrics for a song.

"Asher?"

He cast an apologetic glance her way. "I'm sorry, Maddy, it's been a long day—rough week as a matter of fact—lots going on with Spade. Yes, start as I mean to go on. I was hoping to talk to you about that. I'm not getting enough time with Ella. What do you say we push back her bedtime? I don't usually get home until well after ten most nights, but I'll come home early, say eight-ish, a few nights a week so we can have dinner together and hang out until bedtime."

Her mouth had dropped open during his speech, but it snapped shut with a click. "Are you joking?"

He took another sip of spicy hot chocolate. "No," he said, mildly. "Eight o'clock is a ridiculously early bedtime."

"What time are you proposing?"

"Ten? Ten-thirty?

She let out a shout of laughter.

He frowned. "What's funny?"

"You can't do that, Asher."

He set his jaw. Was she upset because this would wreak havoc on her social life? It wouldn't be every day. "Oh, but I can. You work for me, remember? I know it'll require longer hours—"

"That's not the point."

"I pay overtime."

She had an expression on her face he was sure had been on his many times: amusement combined with disbelief.

"I'm serious, Maddy."

She thumped her mug down on the table. "Asher. How would you feel if I tried to explain management of a successful rock band to you?"

"You said she's adaptable—"

"Not regarding sleep."

He scanned her over the rim of his mug. "We'll try it my way this week. I would like to spend more time with her. We'll do dinner at eight and a ten or ten-thirty bedtime."

She shook her head. "She'll be tired and grumpy and—"

He shrugged. "So, she takes a nap. Kids do that, right?"

She studied him with those serious gray eyes.

His groin tightened.

Damn it.

"I hate like hell to do this to her, but I can see this might be a fairly harmless lesson for you. We'll try it your way. But I want you to be around this week for the fallout."

He straightened. "Fallout?"

"One week. But if we don't last a week your way, you have to promise to be up by seven A.M. and home by six P.M. three days a week from here on in."

Since shifting Ella's schedule would not be the problem Maddy made it out to be, he could agree to a promise that, if upheld, would cast his professional and personal life into chaos.

Maddy held out her hand.

He shook it, and held it.

She froze.

Gently, he turned it so he could see the disfigured joints. He traced the back of her hand, the almost translucent skin, running his thumb over joints that were swollen and warm to the touch. She was close enough that he could smell the heady scent of mint chocolate on her breath.

He made some sound that, knowing her, she probably interpreted as pity.

She yanked her hand away, mumbled goodnight, and fled the kitchen.

• • •

Ella's eyes rolled back, and her lashes fluttered. Her head fell forward in slow motion to land in the salmon, peas, and noodles on her plate.

"My God." Asher put down his utensils, rose from his chair, and rushed to Ella's side.

Maddy continued eating her dinner, making a valiant effort to suppress her grin.

"Maddy," he hissed.

I must not laugh. "Yeah?"

"What's wrong with her?"

"She's exhausted."

His eyes widened. "But…but she passed out mid-sentence. Something's *wrong* with her." He looked at Maddy from his crouch beside Ella. "She's breathing."

"Of course she's breathing. She's just tired."

"What should we do?"

"We should go back to an eight o'clock bedtime."

He groaned. "Damn it."

"Are you agreeable?" Maddy calmly speared a mouthful of salmon on her fork.

"Fine," he said curtly, standing.

"Do you remember the terms?"

His expression was lethal. "Yes."

Maddy put down her utensil and pushed back her chair. She carried her plate to the sink, careful not to show Asher her smug smile.

She walked over to the little girl. "Ella? Ella, honey?" No response but the slow, deep breaths of slumber.

She handed a wet-wipe to Asher and gently levered Ella's head up. He cleaned the child's food-covered face. Ella murmured something unintelligible, her eyes still closed.

"Can you carry her up?" Maddy asked Asher in hushed tones.

He nodded and hefted Ella into his arms. Maddy followed on his heels, grinning. She was glad Asher's little experiment with bedtime hadn't lasted more than four days—and not just because of the concession she'd managed to wring from him. Poor Ella was exhausted. Hell, *she* was exhausted. These last few nights, Ella revved up at nine P.M. and wanted to stay up until eleven.

"Second wind." Maddy's mother had called it when Maddy explained the problem in an e-mail.

Bedtime had become a nightmare. But the real problem was, Ella was so overtired after school she would melt down from four o'clock until dinnertime. Now Asher would have to make time for his niece. And the poor kid was desperate for his attention. He was doing marginally better although he appeared shell-shocked every time Ella mentioned her mother, and he refused to go through his sister's boxes. Maybe she should offer to help? Nah. He'd do it when he was ready.

Chapter 6

The phone conversation with Sterling Lowe haunted Maddy. Her mother's financial situation kept her up at night, but she couldn't give Ella's grandfather what he wanted. It wasn't right. She would keep Asher's parenting struggles to herself. If something major came up, she'd talk to Asher and seek guidance from her mother and Ella's therapist. Not Sterling Lowe. That cure had to be worse than the disease.

She could believe that Sterling wanted what was best for his granddaughter. And there was no doubt that Asher had a steep learning curve in the child-rearing department. The real question was whether Asher had the interest and ability to make a life with the child. Could he prioritize her over Spade—over himself?

Maddy twisted her lips. His progress in that area was incremental—token gestures, increased time at home. But being home more didn't always translate into more time with Ella. It translated into time on the phone, in the study, and in poolside meetings with God knows who all from his industry—mostly suits. If things continued this way, she'd have no choice but to tell the therapist Asher wasn't cutting it as guardian.

Then there was the other problem. She was starting to get what all the fuss was about. Asher was more than charming. He was charismatic. His looks and flirtatiousness were a weapon he had honed to the precision of a deadly blade. Once he pulled it out, manipulation was not far behind. With a sinking feeling, she realized she was attracted to him. When he entered a room, the air snapped and sparkled. Now that he was around more, wearing his body-hugging concert T-shirts and snug jeans, her hormones were in a perpetual state of high alert.

And his reputation as the biggest playboy partier on the planet? Highly exaggerated. There had been no orgies at the house—in fact, no women at all. Of course, he was probably conducting his affairs elsewhere in deference to Ella. But still, he didn't come home reeking of liquor and women, and he rarely drank alcohol at home. Why was she spending time thinking about his sex life? It wasn't as though they'd ever have a relationship outside of the professional one.

Maddy glanced up in surprise from the kitchen table where she was trying to write a paper when she heard clomping on the main staircase. It was early for Asher to be up. Though he had agreed to meet daily to discuss Ella at the psychologist's urging, they had only met twice. The psychologist was clamoring for another meeting, too, but she'd have to get in line.

Asher's step faltered as he spotted her and she leveled him with a stare.

"Maddy." He greeted her heartily, ramping up the smile.

She hastily turned back to her computer screen. Too late, the image was already burned into her retinas. No shirt! He wasn't wearing a shirt. And what were those tattoos? Had the top button of his jeans been undone? *No. Do not check him out again.* His shoulders were broad and thickly muscled—from what? He was a guitarist for heaven's sake. It wasn't like he did heavy lifting. There had been a smattering of hair across his chest that tapered as it made its way into the fly of his jeans, lean hips, and those muscles at the top of his waistband…what were they called? Oh, yeah. Obliques. She stifled a sigh. She wasn't into tatted-up men, she reminded herself. Especially rock superstars. She peeked up as he seated himself at the table across from her, coffee in one hand, banana in the other.

She tried to keep her gaze from sliding down his broad, inked chest. "Asher, we agreed to meet daily."

His smile disappeared. "Is everything okay?"

"Yes and no." Maddy closed her laptop. "This morning Ella had a stomach ache. Last night, a nightmare."

He took a sip from his mug. "Maybe she's sick?"

"The therapist thinks it's anxiety."

There was real fear in those beautiful hazel eyes as they darted away from her study of him.

Maddy refused to let him off the hook. "What's the problem? You hired me to help you care for Maddy, not take *over* care for her. She needs you."

Patience, Maddy.

It was impossible to be around him and not know the kind of pain he was dealing with—the loss of his sister, Ella's meltdowns, nightmares and always, always asking for her mom. He lived here; he had a level of awareness. She'd thought at first he might be depressed. Now she wasn't so sure. Maybe this was just who he was.

She focused on his eyes. Panic. Doubt. They skittered away from hers.

"I've been busy, catching up…"

She waited.

He put down the mug and rested his head in his hands.

She reached across the table.

He took her hand.

Hers tightened in a comforting squeeze. "I'm so sorry. I can't imagine what you are going through. Justin tells me what Dee meant to you, to all of you…It's just that, you know, if you *want* Ella, you have to deal with her. Help her. A lot more than you have been."

His breathing was ragged and he withdrew his hand. "I know. I know. It's just…God! I feel so sorry for her. It rips my heart out to hear her cry, and when she asks for Dee, I feel completely helpless."

"If you're grieving, it's that much harder to comfort her."

He flicked his hand impatiently. "I'm fine. But I have no experience with children. None. And it doesn't come naturally to me."

"Just give her love and attention. That's all she needs from you right now. That and discipline."

He gave a short laugh. "Oh, *that's* all." He took his hand back and ran his hands over his face. "I'll get her from school, take her out after. We'll bring takeout home for dinner, okay?"

"Sure."

Asher rose with his coffee, refilled it, and left the kitchen.

• • •

Maddy was making breakfast an hour later when her cell rang. She glanced at it, annoyed. Asher. She hadn't heard him leave, but that was nothing new, this house was so damn big.

"Maddy? Can you come pick me up, please? Justin's out of town."

"Sure. Where are you?"

"Stunt Road."

"Okay, where on Stunt Road?"

"You can't miss me."

"Did you break down?"

"In a manner of speaking."

"I'll be there in…"

"About an hour, and Maddy?"

"Yes?"

"Drive carefully."

By eleven thirty Maddy was creeping along in her old Honda on the most winding road she'd ever driven, with hundred-foot drops on either side, and only a guardrail between her and death by ravine. Finally, she saw him. Or at least she saw the lights of the patrol car.

Standing on the side of the road was Asher, his Aston Martin wrecked, and at a significant rate of speed by the looks of things. A California Highway Patrol vehicle and a tow truck flanked the damaged automobile. She stared in disbelief out her front windscreen at the scene. Maddy pulled over, put the car in park, and raced over to him.

"Asher!"

"I'm fine, Maddy."

She searched his face, taut with pain.

"Goddamn it, Asher, no you aren't," she gritted. "Officer, if you don't need him for anything, I'm taking him to the closest hospital to get checked out."

The officer's eyebrows arched. "He said he was fine."

She scowled at the two men.

Asher took in her car. "Maddy, this is what you drive?" He was clearly horrified. "It's a deathtrap."

She pointed to his cherry-red sports car, which had mated with the guardrail. "My car is a deathtrap? *My car*? Get in, Asher."

With the help of the CHP officer he seated himself, leaning to close the door with a wince.

"Where's the closest hospital?" she asked.

"Don't need the hospital," Asher said.

"Want me to call an ambulance?" the officer asked.

"How far is it?" she asked, overriding Asher's vehement "God no. No ambulance!"

"Twenty minutes." He pointed east.

"I'll drive him, then," she said.

Thirty minutes later, they reached the hospital. Thirty minutes of listening to an irritable Asher lampoon her car. She was starting to regret giving him a ride.

The hospital scene was the height of absurdity. People in the emergency room waiting room recognized Asher, wanted autographs and tried to chat with him. The ER staff was no better when they brought him back. Despite his injury he was laughing and joking and listening to people reminisce about Spade shows.

"Listen…uh…Miss," she paused to read the name tag of the attractive nurse who had taken Asher aside and was regaling him with her favorite Spade videos, "can you check him out? Or find someone who can?"

Maddy wasn't of the opinion that celebrities should get special treatment—far from it—but Asher was getting paler by the minute and no one seemed to want to evaluate him. The nurse left and a white-haired man in a lab coat, who had no idea what the fuss was about, asked Asher to lie on the table.

Maddy averted her eyes when Asher removed his shirt. He noticed. "Squeamish, Maddy? There's no blood."

She watched him hoist himself up on the table, muscles rippling under golden skin, and felt a surge of lust so powerful she clenched her thighs together as a shiver moved through her.

"Mmmm. I'm sending you for an x-ray. You might have broken a rib or two. If you're lucky it'll just be bruising, which can still cause significant pain," the doctor said.

In short order a group of nurses clustered in the room, ready to walk him back to the lab. Maddy looked heavenward.

Asher handed Maddy his wallet and she took out his ID and insurance card and gave them to the receptionist, who had come in the room.

Thirty minutes after that procedure, the doctor came back, clearing the two nurses from the room. "Mr. Lowe, the good news is nothing is broken. But you're going to be pretty sore for a few days. It shouldn't cause any complications. Rest and you'll heal faster."

• • •

No sooner had they returned to the Honda when Asher started up again about her car.

"Asher. You're pissing me off," Maddy snapped.

Asher shifted on the seat and tugged on the vinyl belt across his chest. "Tough."

"It has airbags, great fuel economy, it's reliable—"

"No."

"What do you mean, 'No'? It's my car. Listen, Mr. Silver Spoon—"

"*You* listen. I lost my sister in a crash."

Maddy spared him a glance. Amazing how quickly he could go from charming and flirtatious with the emergency room staff to irritable and angry with her.

He was practically snarling, his hands fisted in his lap. "I'm not going to have you riding around in this...this...car," he ground out. "I won't have it." He shook his head and half turned, grimacing in pain. "I can't believe I didn't notice."

Maddy watched him out of the corner of her eye.

He scanned the rear and spotted Ella's car seat. "And Ella has been riding around in *this*? Unacceptable."

Maddy clenched her teeth together and pulled off the freeway and into a gas station. She put the car in park with a shaking hand and turned off the ignition, seething.

"You outta gas?"

She turned toward him in the seat. "What the hell is wrong with you?"

"Me?"

"Yes. Out on *that* road in *that* car, going way too fast. You don't get to have a death wish. It's not about you anymore, Asher, or hadn't you noticed? You're now responsible for the life of a *child*. You don't get to be reckless. You don't get to avoid her. Not if you want to keep her."

His lips pressed together so tightly they were nearly white. She couldn't see his eyes behind the sunglasses, but his face was set, rigid. "Who do you think *you* are, threatening me?"

"Who do you think you are to lecture *me* about the safety of my car? *Me!* I drive like a freaking ninety-year-old on tranquilizers when I have Ella in the backseat. I'm sick of it. I've only been here two weeks…" Her breath caught on an angry sob and she turned away from him to stare out the windshield. "And I'm not even sure what I'm doing. I don't know how to help her with her grief, and you're…*unavailable*." She dashed away angry tears and then turned the key, and the engine came to life.

Asher reached over and covered her hand on the steering wheel, grimacing at the movement. "Okay," he said, softly. "You're right. I'm sorry."

She shot him a look. "Asher, I'm just the help. She's your family. And yes, this car is fifteen years old, but it's paid for, and given my student loans, I'm not sure I can get a loan for—"

Asher groaned. "Maddy, I'm not asking *you* to buy a car. I know you're not in a position to do that."

Oh, yeah. He'd had her checked out. He knew she didn't have two cents to rub together and a boatload of debt.

"You want me to use one of your cars?" She pulled out of the gas station and back onto the freeway.

"Hell, no. My cars aren't known for their safety records. Most of them don't even have a rear seat."

Asher tapped at his phone with an air of distraction for a few minutes, and then made a call.

"Justin? Asher. I wrecked the Aston Martin on Stunt Drive.

California Highway Patrol may be calling you, or a tow company, possibly the media. Yes, yes, I'm fine. Maddy took me to get checked out."

There was shouting from the other end of the phone and Asher pulled it away from his ear. She snuck a glance, wide-eyed.

"I've already been given an effective lecture, Justin. Done?" There was a pause. "Yes. Good. Now I need you to get me a Mercedes for Maddy to drive, preferably a ML350 SUV. Loaded. Color?" He grinned. "Red. Hell, yes, I'm serious. Have you seen what she drives? I'm not having her drive my niece around in that. See ya." Asher tried to put the phone in his pocket, grunted in pain, then gave up and put it on the console.

Life was so unfair. She couldn't pay her mom's twenty thousand dollar debt yet she'd be driving around a car that likely cost twice that.

"Asher, I am not driving a Mercedes. It's excessive and…and ostentatious!"

"It's one of the safest vehicles on the road. End of discussion." He ignored her protests for two full minutes before he spoke up again. "Maddy, you will not win this argument."

She braked for a light and couldn't help noticing that he put a hand to his head.

She was quiet the rest of the ride.

Later that afternoon, a car dealer dropped off the SUV. He even installed Ella's car seat. Burgundy on the outside—the closest to red they had without special ordering—it had a rounded dashboard with wood paneling and leather. The seats were a neutral crème, pure elegance, and Maddy hated it on sight.

• • •

Asher leaned against the kitchen counter with a full mug of hot chocolate, reveling in the warm, golden glow of the early morning light coming through the windows and watching Maddy go about her morning routine with Ella. He hadn't been up this early regularly in…well, ever. And he found himself enjoying his revised schedule, watching and occasionally participating in the preparations for the day, which included gummy vitamins, a breakfast bar, and a packed lunch. Ella had been living here six weeks, Maddy four. She was a miracle worker.

"Ella, get your shoes, honey," Maddy said, crossing over to Asher with a smile as she put the dishes in the sink.

His niece brought her lace-up sneakers, and sat on the kitchen chair as Maddy crouched down in front of her to tie them.

Maddy kept up a steady stream of banter about school the entire time.

Curious, Asher walked over to the table and peered over her shoulder. What was taking so long? Maddy attempted to tie the shoelaces again. Then again. He studied her thin hands with their red, swollen knuckles, some of the fingers on her right hand off kilter. An involuntary sound escaped him.

She cast a quelling look over her shoulder.

He crouched next to her. "Let me," he said, reaching for Ella's foot.

Maddy held it away from him. "No, I'll do it."

Ella's wide-eyed, brown gaze darted from one adult to the other.

Maddy sighed. "Please, Asher."

It was obvious her hands were stiff, probably painful, and he was surprised by her lack of dexterity. He rarely thought about her condition anymore. It didn't seem to affect her. But now, watching her struggle, his chest grew tight.

She finished tying the first shoe.

Asher reached to take the second shoe from her, aware of Ella's curious gaze.

"Asher." She met his eyes calmly. "Ella can see that I have trouble tying her laces, especially in the morning, but I try until I get it, right Ella?"

"Right, Maddy."

He sat back on his heels, his throat thickening as she put the shoe on the little foot with her swollen, gnarled hands. It took her two laborious attempts to tie the laces.

She glanced up into his face and whispered, "It's okay."

He rose to his feet.

But it wasn't okay. There were those reports from his investigator. Apparently she'd left college between her junior and senior years due to health problems. Mrs. Anderson had spent a small fortune in medical bills. Medical bills that had led to a bankruptcy and ongoing financial problems. Was Maddy having a flare-up of the disease? He knew what rheumatoid arthritis was, or he thought he did. He'd researched it soon after meeting her on the plane because he needed to be sure it wouldn't get in the way of caring for Ella. So far it hadn't. Until this morning, he hadn't realized the million little things that were difficult for her. There must be *something* that could be done.

He snapped his attention back to the scene in the kitchen as he realized Maddy was speaking to him. "Asher, will you take Ella to the bus stop this morning?"

He nodded and held out his hand to help Maddy up. He ran his thumb over the tops of her small hands. Hands that must give her pain.

She scowled and tugged it away. "Don't pity me," she hissed.

"I don't pity you," he replied, his eyes searching hers, astonished by the tenderness that swept through him. "Does it hurt?"

She cut her gaze to Ella, gave a quick negative shake of her head, and then turned to grab Ella's lunch from the counter.

"Backpack," she reminded, following them to the front door. She kissed Ella on the cheek and knelt to give her a hug. "Have a good day, honey."

"Can we go for frozen yogurt after school?"

"We'll see."

Ella's face fell and she whispered to Asher, "That means no."

Maddy smiled. "It means maybe."

It was impossible to keep pace with a five-year-old. She was either skipping ahead or dawdling behind, all the while keeping up a steady stream of chatter about her reading buddy, a fourth grader named Olive, and what she wanted Santa to bring her for Christmas. Christmas! It wasn't even Thanksgiving. In the past, he'd taken off and headed to Cabo or Hawaii with a girlfriend or group of friends. Last year he'd taken someone—Natasha, if memory served—to a tiny island in the South Pacific; he had vague memories of scuba diving, sailing, and squabbles.

Family holidays were out of the question after that disastrous Vegas Christmas three years ago. Dee had spent half of the time pleading with him to stop baiting his father, and the other half telling Sterling to quit being so argumentative. Asher had made an effort—the first day. But the continual tension had left them all on edge and he'd flown back to L.A. before things could come to a head with the old man. His stomach churned. If only Dee hadn't reconciled with Sterling. If only he'd had more time with her.

This year he'd be celebrating with someone who still believed in Santa. He made a mental note to talk to Justin about getting a tree, lights, ornaments—the whole shebang. It would be lonely with just him and Ella, since Justin and his partner had plans to go on a cruise that week and Maddy was going home to Virginia.

Asher walked up the steps to his house, entered, and closed the front door. He was going to trash every last pair of lace-up shoes Ella owned and replace them with ones with Velcro. After he made a phone call.

He came down the stairs thirty minutes later and deposited the paper bag with three pairs of lace up shoes near the front door. "Maddy?"

She stepped out of the living room into the hallway, a mug in hand.

"Can we talk? I have a couple of things I want to discuss with you."

"Sure." She followed him across the gleaming wood floor to the enormous chocolate suede sectional and tucked herself into the corner.

Had she winced just then?

He seated himself a foot away, turning to study her. Odd. When he'd met her on the plane, he could have sworn she wasn't beautiful. Barely pretty. Now? He was…attracted. No, more than that. His body rebelled against this ridiculous celibacy with surges of lust toward her at utterly inappropriate times. He'd never met anyone less inclined to play the temptress, and yet, everything, every move she made, was enticing. Was it because he couldn't have her? Was he so used to getting whatever he wanted that now he only wanted what he couldn't have? He grimaced. If that was the case, he was pretty fucked up.

He'd been out a handful of times in the last few weeks and hadn't jumped in bed with anyone. He didn't want to bring anyone here and he couldn't seem to work up enough interest to take a woman to a hotel. Maybe he needed to hit some better parties or clubs. Then there was the getting up early thing. He didn't feel as disconnected as he had the first few weeks after Dee's death. Maybe he was coming out of his funk.

Maddy was far too thin for his liking, but her thick-lashed, wide-spaced, sober gray eyes, that nearly perfect bone structure, those lips…his gaze lingered on her lips. She smiled over the rim of her mug and his heart skipped a beat. There it was, that magnificent smile. *That* was what made her beautiful. Now that she was living here and he was spending more time with her and Ella, he got to see that smile frequently. Sure, her lips triggered lust, but that wasn't what seized up his heart. He had plenty of experience with lust. This was…tenderness, affection. Combined with lust it was uncomfortable and, given their situation, completely inappropriate. She was his employee, for God's sake.

"Let's talk about your…condition," he said.

Her smile vanished, leaving a frozen, expressionless mask in its wake.

"What are you doing for it, medically speaking?"

"None of your business," she responded frostily.

"I made an appointment with a rheumatologist," he ignored her gasp, "the best in the area, to talk about treatment options."

Her gaze was stony. "Asher, I manage my disease. I have since I was a teenager," she replied, frost giving way to ice.

"Are you on the latest medications?"

She dropped her gaze. "I'm on…a medication. It helps."

"Are there other, better options? What about physical therapy?"

"Asher, I'm not comfortable talking about this. You're my boss."

"Tough," he responded. "I need you to be healthy to…to take care of Ella."

Her eyes flashed. "I am healthy, damn it." She twisted her hands together in her lap.

"I know it's a chronic illness. I've read a little bit about it."

Her chin came up.

"I read there are some pretty powerful medications. I also know that if you decide to try them you need regular follow-up with a doctor and shots or intravenous infusions. You haven't done any of that, as far as I know, since I've met you."

Her eyes narrowed and her lips pressed together so tightly the skin around her lips blanched.

He went on doggedly, "If you need any of those things, our insurance is good, and what it doesn't cover, I will."

"You don't need to—"

"Bullshit." He moved closer to her. "I want to understand. Are there drugs you could take to make it less painful, less—"

"Ugly?"

"No." He took her hand in his. "It's not ugly, Maddy. Nothing about you is ugly." He swallowed and released her hand. "It's hard to watch you struggle. It's hard to know someone like you is in pain."

She looked daggers at him with those magnificent gray eyes. "Someone like me?"

"Someone I care about, someone Ella loves."

She sighed. "Asher, the newer medications are expensive; some aren't even covered. And some of the damage to my joints happened during my childhood before those drugs were available, so I have scar tissue that interferes with my dexterity. Then there are the side effects…its trial and error."

"This better not be about money."

She laughed, but it was bitter. "Easy for you to say, Richie Rich. It *is* about money. I'm a part-time student and a full-time employee. If the insurance company covers the medications at all, it won't cover the full amount and they're really expensive— we're talking thousands of dollars. And don't get me started on the expense of doctor visits for follow-up and hospital visits if there are complications. Believe me, I speak from experience."

"But there are benefits? To the newer medications?"

"They can slow the progression of the disease. They can reduce pain," she admitted. "But they make me more susceptible to infection, complications from colds and flu viruses. Let's not forget we live with a little germ factory." She managed a smile.

There was that hitch in his chest again.

"I want you to keep that appointment, Maddy. Please. Let's see what the insurance covers; it's supposed to be a good plan."

She stood up. "Fine."

"And I want you to do whatever he recommends. Expense and complications be damned."

She shook her head. "And if I get sick?"

"We'll take care of you."

• • •

Maddy scowled as she sat in the front passenger seat of the luxury sports car—this one was even more ridiculous than the one he wrecked, if that was possible. People stared at it in the stop-and-go traffic on the freeway. Clearly Asher, who had insisted on driving her to her doctor's appointment, didn't believe in keeping a low profile. They discussed Maddy and her classes on the way, but Maddy was too annoyed to relax. She was also nervous about meeting with the rheumatologist.

After the complete physical exam, the doctor instructed her to dress and meet him in his office.

She sat in one of the two chairs facing his desk. The door opened and Asher came in the room. Her mouth dropped open as he settled himself into the chair next to her.

"What are you doing?" she asked. This conversation would be difficult enough without her rock star boss hanging on every word, waiting to take over her decisions. She'd stopped allowing her mother into her consults as soon as she turned eighteen. This disease was hers to manage. Her pain. Her choices.

"Finding out what I need to do to help," he replied, giving her a smile that nearly stopped her heart.

She ignored that traitorous organ, allowing anger to stiffen her spine. "Asher, get out. This is none of your business and totally inappropriate."

"I know," he replied. "I just want to know what we can do—"

"*You* can't do anything. I'm not a child, I've been managing my disease—"

"Oh really?" He raised an eyebrow. "Is that what the doctor is going to say? That your disease is well-managed? I need to know as your employer and your friend that we are doing everything we can."

"The doctor is not going to tell *you* anything, Asher Lowe. Now get out!"

The doctor knocked on the door and entered.

"Doctor, you are not allowed to share any of my medical information with this man. In fact, I don't want you to speak while he's in the room," Maddy said.

"Maddy." Asher's tone was pleading.

Tough. His manipulations would not work with her.

"Asher. I'll admit I've let some things slide. Mainly due to time, money, benefits." She shrugged. "But if this job allows, I'll follow the doctor's recommendations for drug and non-drug treatment to the letter. Go wait for me in the waiting room."

The doctor started to interrupt, but Maddy silenced him. "Not one word, doctor, while he's here."

Asher stood, his expression stony, and left the room.

The rheumatologist grinned. "Must be nice."

"*Nice?*"

"To have someone care that much," he said, still grinning.

Maddy stiffened. "We're not together, if that's what you're alluding to."

"Oh, no." Dr. Baxter lost his smile. "I never thought so."

Of course not. The idea of Asher Lowe with Madeline Anderson was inconceivable.

The doctor recommended one of the newer biologics to treat her disease. He warned that if she got sick, she could end up hospitalized with complications, so he needed to see her monthly for follow-up visits.

"Maddy, when was the last time you had a flare?"

"I've had some minor ones along the way, but the last significant one was in college."

"How bad?"

"Pretty bad. I had to drop out for two semesters. There were a few hospitalizations that year."

But that hadn't been the worst thing. The worst thing that year was Trey. Who could blame him? She didn't. Not anymore. She'd gotten sick—really sick—her junior year in college. And Trey couldn't deal with endless doctor visits, the hospital stays, caring for her after her discharge. Trey was fun-loving and clever, he had loved her—of that she had no doubt—but he was not equipped to deal with her illness. She had broken up with him, beating him to the punch, and remembering the relief mixed with guilt in his eyes when she told him they were done. The hollow protestations of love, loyalty, and support that followed. Her stomach churned at the memory. So she had returned home and had another flare, and then another, and it was a year before she had the stamina to return to college.

"So that's good then," the doctor said, as he made a notation in her chart, "the significant flares have been infrequent. I'll know more after I run your lab work, but you seem to be pretty healthy, considering."

Maddy nodded.

"We're going to change up your medications. I'll go over what that will mean, but I also have a list here of non-drug treatments." He glanced up from his paperwork "If you do them routinely, they'll help."

"Exercise?" Maddy asked wearily. Working as a barista and being on her feet all day, classes, and studying had left neither the time nor the inclination for exercise other than walking the last few years.

"Yes. Swimming is best. Can you swim?"

She nodded.

"Does Mr. Lowe have a pool?"

"Yeah. Heated year-round," she admitted.

"That'll be perfect. Hot tub?"

She smirked and he laughed. "I'll take that as an 'of course.'"

He encouraged physical therapy twice a week and they worked up a schedule of stretching, swimming, and hot-tub soaks.

They shook hands and Maddy went out to the waiting room to schedule her next appointment. She was surprised to see Asher leaning on the counter, chatting with the front office staff—all women, all eating out of his hand. She cleared her throat. One of the ladies hustled over to schedule her next visit.

Asher winked.

Once in the car, she caught Asher sneaking glances. "Okay, okay. I'll tell you what he recommended."

"Oh, the nurses were very forthcoming about the typical treatments for your condition."

"Stop calling it that. Seriously, Asher, its rheumatoid arthritis. Not 'my disease' or 'my condition.' And I'll do what the doctor suggested; I'm no masochist."

"Good."

"Stop butting in though. I mean it."

"Okay." He sounded duly chastened, but he was smiling.

She smothered an answering grin.

• • •

The next morning, after walking Ella to the bus stop, Maddy put on her blue swimsuit, a piece so old and dry-rotted it was almost transparent. She studied herself in the mirror ruefully. No, not almost transparent…actually transparent. Had it been that long since she'd been swimming? Yikes. This thing was indecent. It was time to order a new suit with rush delivery.

She pulled her hair into a tight ponytail, wrapped herself in one of Asher's many white guest robes and made her way downstairs.

The water was steaming, and it was a chilly fall morning. Her feet were freezing, and after she took off the robe and threw it in a lounge chair, the rest of her was, too. She gave a brief longing look at the hot tub, then entered the pool water. Not warm enough. She stood uncertainly, halfway down the steps of the long rectangular pool, and trailed her fingers in the water, dreading the moment she would have to immerse herself. The hair on the back of her neck prickled, and she glanced up to the window of the master suite, Asher's room.

There he was in the huge window, staring down, wearing what appeared to be a towel wrapped around his hips. His eyes were locked on her, not moving. She dropped her gaze, then remembered her transparent suit and plunged the rest of the way down the steps to start her laps, her mind racing. Why had he been standing there, staring?

• • •

After dinner, she approached her room to find, hanging on the doorknob, a bag from a sporting goods store. She unhooked the purchase and brought it into her bedroom, bemused. She shut the door and reached in, retrieving a pair of goggles and an orange rubber swim cap. That was thoughtful of him. The paper still hung heavy in her hand—she peeked inside and grabbed the silky black material lying at the bottom. Huh. A swimsuit. She checked the tags. Her size. She held it up, flipped it around and cocked her head. The style could politely be called matronly. Once on, it would cover most of her chest and back and all of her hips. It was not flattering, not in the slightest. It wasn't like she had plans to buy a bikini—she was swimming for exercise after all—but this thing was hideous. The memory of him standing motionless in the window and wearing only a towel popped into her head.

Chapter 7

"Uncle Asher? Where are those people going with those dogs?"

Distracted from his Saturday morning mission to obtain the latest gaming device, he looked up from his smartphone. "Hmmm? Oh, there's a pet shop in here somewhere."

"A pet shop?" Ella's eyes lit up. "Can I go there?"

He glanced at her, tugging on his hand. "Yeah. Sure," he murmured absently. "But I need to get this console. You'll like it, Ella." Or he hoped she would. Maddy had suggested it might be a good thing to bond over. He wasn't a video gamer. Not that he hadn't battled friends in the Rock God guitar game to kill time on the road. But dancing? Bowling? Tennis? He shuddered. Still, if Maddy thought it would help, he was willing to try.

He also needed to get Ella a bike with training wheels. Maddy had been full of suggestions for strengthening their relationship after the therapist told him she'd like to see more of a connection between him and his niece.

He pulled her into the electronics store and caught the wistful look she cast over her shoulder.

"Ella, I'm here to buy a game console for you," he said, mildly exasperated.

"Yeah, but I'd really like to have a cat," she said, peering up with sad, brown eyes.

Just as he made it to the right section of the store, his phone rang. Justin. He let go of Ella's hand to answer. "Yeah?"

"Asher. Peter Shay called twice this morning. Something about studio time? He hates to bug you, but he's not able to resolve it."

When would he learn that no good deed goes unpunished?

He had an interest in a few fledgling bands with talent and tried to help them up through the ranks. Getting studio time in any city without much money or clout was always problematic.

"I don't suppose you—"

Justin sighed. "I can try, but you know how they are in Philly. Whereas one call from you—"

"Yeah, yeah. Send me the particulars. I'll try to get it done." He reached the right aisle, tucked the phone away, and turned to ask his niece which games she preferred.

No Ella.

He scanned his immediate area. No sign of her.

Annoyed, he walked over to a man outfitted in the store's hallmark blue-and-orange shirts.

"Did you see a little girl?"

The man stared, his mouth opened.

Fuck. He knew that expression, the "hey, aren't you…" pause.

"Never mind," Asher said.

His long strides chewed up the aisles as a chill went up his spine. Where was she?

Within five minutes, he'd been through the whole store at an Indianapolis 500 pace. Irritation was replaced by panic and fear. His hands shook.

My God.

He approached a male employee a few feet away.

"Where's your manager?" he barked.

The sullen kid pointed in the direction of the televisions lining the wall.

Halting, he pulled out his phone and dialed with trembling fingers.

"Maddy?"

"Hey."

"I've lost Ella."

"*What? Where?*"

"I'm in Fry's, the electronics store."

"Okay. How long has she been gone?"

"About five minutes."

"And you've searched the store?"

"Yeah. She's not here."

"Don't those stores have a guy at the front who verifies purchases?"

"Brilliant, Maddy." He hung up on her and charged to the front.

"Hey." He grabbed the bored employee standing at the exit doors by the arm. "Did you see a little girl come by here?"

The man pulled away, astonishment at being touched warring with irritation on his young, acned face. "Yeah. A few minutes ago."

"Where'd she go?"

"She asked me how to get to the pet store."

Asher's eyes bore into the man, fear giving way to terror. *She'd left the store?*

His phone rang.

"Which way is it?"

The man pointed east. Asher dug his cell out of his pocket. "Yeah?"

Justin started to speak.

"Later," Asher barked, hanging up.

His heart raced. The phone rang again in his hand before he had a chance to tuck it back into his pocket.

Maddy. He answered as he broke into a run down the sidewalk of the strip mall. That massive pet store was two, or was it three doors down?

"Did you find her?"

"Not yet, but I think she went into Pet Smart—it's at the other end."

"Call me back when you know something. I'm scared, Asher."

"Me too." He hung up and put the phone back in his pocket as he entered the store. What was Ella wearing? He racked his brain. Pink, of course. Probably purple as well. He couldn't for the life of him remember what, but she *always* wore only those two colors. He needed to talk to Maddy about changing up her attire. It wasn't normal for a kid to be that limited. Even if Maddy thought they were good colors on Ella, would it kill her to add a little blue or green to the child's wardrobe?

He spotted an older man in a white shirt with a gold nametag talking with a cashier at an empty checkout lane.

"Excuse me. My niece came in here alone, and I need help finding her."

"Of course, sir." The two men came over to his side of the register.

The man with thinning hair and a gold nameplate proclaiming "Jerry: Manager" studied him. "How old is she?"

"Five."

He nodded. "Her name?"

"Ella."

"What's she wearing?"

"Pink and purple."

The man grinned. "Oh, I remember my own going through that phase."

Asher stared, uncomprehending.

"Dave, go stand by the front door. No one leaves the store with a young child until we find her. Just ask them to wait. Okay?" Without waiting for an answer, Jerry continued to take charge. "I'll take this side. You take the other."

Asher was already hustling toward the aisles.

He spotted her in the third row. Relief made him lightheaded, and he rested his hands on his thighs. Anger overpowered relief. His fists clenched. How could she do this to him? He didn't trust himself not to yell, so he stayed a few feet away, watching.

She was on tiptoe, leaning over a partition, expression rapt.

The manager approached from the other side of the store and halted when Asher pointed a finger at Ella.

The man nodded and came over to stand next to him.

"It's always the kittens or the puppies."

Asher raised a trembling hand to his sweaty brow. "Why would she just take off like that?"

The man cocked his head. "You know their impulse control at this age isn't the greatest."

No, this was the first he'd heard of that.

"I had four of my own." He patted Asher on the back. "It doesn't get any easier."

Asher groaned. "I'm new to this," he admitted. "I never thought she'd take off."

"Well, the allure of the kitten…"

Asher half-laughed. "I was next door trying to buy her a Wii."

"A pet is better than a Wii, not that you can't have both."

Asher froze. "Oh, no. No animals."

"Why not?"

Memory stirred. He couldn't have been much older than Ella when he had begged his father for a cat, a dog—anything. Too messy, Sterling had said, and far too inconvenient. As he got older, he stopped wishing for a pet and started playing guitar, then electric guitar. They weren't messy or inconvenient. Just loud.

Maybe the best thing for Ella would be something to love and care for in the wake of her mom's death.

The manger glanced over. "Uh oh," he said, with a smile.

"Maybe a puppy…"

"My advice?"

The guy had raised four kids and ran a pet store. That must make him *some* kind of expert.

"We have some rescue cats. Much lower maintenance than dogs, and with adult cats you pretty much know what kind of personality you get. We have a few sweethearts who are desperate for a good home. Not a puppy or a dog if you're still new to the parenting thing. Not if you," he glanced meaningfully at Asher, "travel a lot."

So much for the ball cap and sunglasses.

Asher reached out to shake his hand. "Asher Lowe."

"Jerry Grodin. Big fan. Let's get you set up, shall we?"

Moments later, Asher texted Maddy to let her know all was well. It was too late. They were picking out supplies when Maddy dashed in, wearing sweat pants, her hair yanked back in a messy ponytail.

He smiled and walked over.

She cast a worried glance at Ella, who was debating the various attributes of cat trees with the manager.

"What happened?"

He sighed and ran through the story, watching her body stiffen.

"And she just walked away? And you didn't notice?"

Asher shuffled his feet. "Justin called about something. I was distracted, just for a few minutes—"

"Asher!"

"I know. *I know.*"

"We need to talk to her about this."

"Already done."

Her eyes narrowed suspiciously as Ella help Jerry pull a litter box from the shelf.

"What's going on?"

"We thought a cat—"

She shook her head. "No, no, no."

"Hear me out."

"No, Asher, no."

He took her upper arm. "Are you allergic? Is it a problem with your disease?" He hadn't even considered that. *Stupid.*

"No. But cats require care and—"

"I'll take care of it. I'll find a reliable pet sitter. You'll see. I think having something to love," grief welled within him, "might help." His voice hoarsened and Maddy had that look in her eyes again, compassion mixed with pity.

"All right," she said, softly. "Maybe we could use a pet in our lives. Not a kitten, right?"

"Right. They have some cats in the back that Jerry says," she looked confused and he pointed at the manager, now picking out a pink-and-purple collar set, "might work well for our family."

Our family. He froze. Had he just said "our family"?

Maddy nodded; she hadn't noticed.

"Do you want to go to the back and check them out while we finish up here?"

"Sure," she said, ruffling Ella's hair as she walked by.

"Maddy!" Ella grabbed her in an ungentle hug. "We're getting a *cat!*"

Maddy grinned down at his niece and his heart flipped.

Chapter 8

"I don't know why we're going to his house. River never plays with me at school," Ella said.

Maddy steered the big, burgundy Mercedes down the palm tree–lined street, past all the enormous houses, the immaculately manicured lawns and, of course, the giant gates. Ah, there it was, three one three.

"What, honey?" Maddy asked absently, with a brief look in the rear-view mirror at Ella. Ella's arms were folded across her chest, her lower lip stuck out mutinously.

Maddy sighed as she pulled in the driveway. It was going to be that kind of day, was it? She rolled down the window and pushed the intercom buzzer.

"Hello?" A tinny voice sang out.

"Hi…uh…it's Maddy and Ella."

"Who?" Annoyance laced with impatience came through the speaker.

"Maddy and Ella. From school. We have a play date with River."

"Just a moment."

Maddy tapped her fingers on the steering wheel and kept her foot firmly on the brake.

"Why are we even here? I don't *like* River."

Maddy put the car in park and half turned in her seat. "You don't?"

"No, he doesn't—"

"*He?* I thought River was a girl."

Ella frowned and then giggled. "Maddyyy, River's a boy!"

She tilted her head. "Then why are we here?" Not that Ella couldn't have a play date with a boy, but at this age, obsessed as she was with princess-play and ponies, it was doubtful she and River would have much common ground. She bit back a groan. Turning back to the black intercom, Maddy pushed the button. "Hello? Hello?"

They waited for five more minutes. She pulled two Barbie dolls from her cavernous purse and handed them back to Ella.

"Maddy, let's go hooome," Ella whined. "I'd rather play with you."

The therapist had advised as much socialization as possible. Being the new girl at a school where nearly all the children had attended preschool together couldn't be easy for Ella. Play dates and parties were top of the therapist's list for helping children assimilate. Maddy pressed the button again and again, holding it down. She glanced at her watch; it had been nearly ten minutes.

"Hellooo?" the same voice sang out.

"We're still here."

"Oh, yeah. Mrs. Reed is still…er…indisposed. Just a moment."

"Can you buzz us in?"

"Uh…I'm not sure. Mrs. Reed is very careful—"

Maddy scowled. "I have a five-year-old child here. Mrs. Reed set up the play date. Just buzz us in."

"I have to pee," came a small the voice from the back seat.

Maddy's eyes widened.

"*Now.*"

She pressed the intercom buzzer. No response.

Damn it!

Unbuckling her seat belt, she grabbed the wipes from her purse.

She cast a glance up and down the street. Barely a bush to use as cover. The whole place was wall-to-wall gates and fences.

Ella's eyes were round brown pools of concern.

Maddy forced a smile. "Hey, Ella. Dogs do it outside. Even adults go outside when they go camping. Don't worry."

"Outside? What if someone sees me?" Her eyes narrowed suspiciously. "Adults go outside?"

"Sure. When they're camping. I'll hide you." She silently rained curses down on Mrs. Reed as she helped Ella pull off her leggings, underwear, and shoes, leading her over to the tiny bush along the wall. A car passed, and slowed, then another.

"Maddy," she hissed, tearfully.

The coast was clear. "Okay. Okay." She helped Ella squat in the grass next to the sidewalk and held her dress up high enough that it wouldn't get wet, and wouldn't expose her. Success. Or close enough.

Maddy helped her back into her clothes and Ella viewed the mess, wide-eyed. "Are we just going to leave it there?"

"Yep. Some dog will come along and pee on it."

The child giggled.

After she had Ella safely in her seat, Maddy cleaned her hands with another wipe, then disinfected with hand sanitizer. Climbing back into the driver's seat, she put the car in reverse.

Screw them.

The box squawked "Hello? Ella? Ella?"

Maddy put the car in park. "Yes, we're still here."

"I'm terribly sorry about the wait—" She was interrupted by screeching. "No, no, nooooo. I don't want her—"

The intercom went silent.

Maddy and Ella exchanged glances in the rearview mirror.

Maddy pushed the button. "Sounds like this isn't a great time." She put the big car in reverse.

The soft tsking sound of Ella sucking her thumb came from the backseat. Maddy's brow furrowed. She'd been the nanny long enough to know this was a sign of stress or fatigue in her charge— and there was no reason Ella should be tired. Was she pushing Ella too hard? Was she scarred for life by having to pee on the roadside?

Maybe I'm not cut out for this. I've got input from the therapist, teachers, my mom, and I still feel like I'm failing this kid.

Chapter 9

Asher's first evening alone with Ella since Maddy had come to stay with them would be easy. He was standing in the foyer when Maddy arrived downstairs and he got a whiff of her. Perfume. She didn't ordinarily wear it, and he wrinkled his nose. It was a nice scent, lightly floral, but he preferred her usual, natural scent. Wait—he knew what she usually smelled like?

Her hair fell in gentle waves past her shoulders, gleaming. A short mini-skirt hugged her body and was topped off by a tight, lacy, gray-blue camisole peeking out from the form-fitting cashmere hoodie. Tall boots with a low heel completed the outfit. He couldn't keep the disapproval from his face.

"Something wrong?" Maddy asked as she approached him.

He shook his head.

Maddy twisted her fingers nervously.

"Asher, are you sure…" her voice trailed off as she caught his expression and she laughed.

"I know. I know. You can handle one five-year-old girl." She smiled and his heart rate doubled.

What was wrong with him?

Why did he keep having to remind himself she was off limits? He liked her for Christ's sake. More than that, he needed her. Ella loved her. The libido would stay in check. There were plenty of women available to him, but Madeline Anderson was not one of them.

"Have a great time. We will," he said dismissively, turning on his heel.

He stalked into the kitchen where Ella was coloring at the table.

She looked up. "Has Maddy left?"

"She's in the hallway."

Ella scooted out of her chair and rushed to find her. The child returned moments later smiling, resumed her seat, and finished coloring her picture, singing to herself.

He opened the fridge to find his Coke and sitting on the top shelf was a plate with plain chicken, brown rice, and broccoli covered in plastic wrap, a note on top.

The note instructed him to zap the plate in the microwave for thirty seconds. He rolled his eyes, grabbed the soda, poured it out into a glass sitting on the island and found another note.

"Bedtime: eight P.M."

He balled it up and considered setting the damn thing on fire. She didn't give him any credit. Then again, he *had* made a mess of things the first few weeks. He still wouldn't win any parenting awards, but he was improving. He didn't need a series of notes coaching him.

"Ella, want to go out for dinner?"

Her eyes lit up. "Pizza?"

"Steak?"

She considered him. "With ketchup?"

"Ketchup," he agreed, shuddering. It was criminal the way the child adulterated food.

He glanced at his watch. Almost six. They'd leave in a few minutes. He'd just brought the soda to his lips when his phone rang. He inspected his screen. Ah, Spade's new producer. He'd been anticipating this call all day. "Ella, want to watch a show?"

He took the call as he set up the TV program for her in the living room.

When he finally got off the phone, he glanced at his watch again. Almost an hour had passed. He collected Ella and her jacket, pulled on his own then snagged his keys and phone. They were finally sitting down at the restaurant close to eight. Ella was complaining and he remembered what Maddy had said about kids getting hungry, so he asked the waiter for some rolls.

The rolls arrived but one glance told him Ella wouldn't eat them. They had seeds. Her whining amplified. He stopped another server.

"Dude, got any plain rolls, bread…*anything* plain?"

"Something wrong with the rolls?" He picked up the basket and examined them.

Ella's tears began and with them came the attention of most of the restaurant patrons. He glanced up and caught glares from the well-coiffed older couple at the next table. He scanned the room. No other kids. He was *that* guy now. The guy who tainted fine dining ambiance with a whiny kid.

He opened a sugar packet and leaned across the table to pour it into Ella's mouth. Her tears dried up. Ah, the magic of sugar. He'd poured eight sugar packets into her mouth by the time their food arrived. He pretended not to notice the withering looks from the people sitting around him as the mountain of empty sugar packets grew in front of him.

He was halfway through his meal when he noticed Ella pushing food around on her plate. "I don't like it." Her eyes drooped a bit at the corners and he glanced at his watch. Approaching nine. He set to finishing his meal, accompanied by the increased fretting of his dinner companion. To quiet her down, he ordered a soda.

She sucked it down in a minute flat, giggled and belched, then groaned and gripped her stomach. Belched again.

Fork halfway to his lips, he watched her mouth form a perfect O of surprise as a fountain of Coke, sugar, and bile spewed onto her shirt, plate, and tablecloth.

Dropping his utensil, he moved to her side. She was sobbing uncontrollably. Jesus. What a mess. He reached in his back pocket;

pulled a few hundreds out of his money clip to drop on the table; gathered the tiny, sticky, smelly figure into his arms and headed for the restaurant door.

Once home, he stripped off her clothes and put her in a warm bath. By the time she was out and dressed in her pajamas, it was after ten and she could barely keep her eyes open.

"Uncle Asher, stay with me," she insisted sleepily, eyes listless with fatigue.

He stripped off his shirt, toed off his shoes and laid on top of the covers next to her, listening to her suck her thumb, blanket in hand as she faded off into sleep. He was aware of her warm body, snuggled in close, the strawberry scented shampoo, the intermittent sucking noises. He closed his eyes, drowsy in the dark room, and smiled. Ella brought out every protective instinct he had ever experienced and turned it up to eleven. He thought he loved his sister's child before, but that was nothing compared to how much he loved her now. Not a day went by that he didn't mourn the loss of Dee, but lately, being with Ella erased some of the grief and brought solace. He hadn't realized how much one person could care for another until Ella came to stay.

• • •

Maddy arrived back at the house after midnight. Her friends had met her at a restaurant near campus before heading out to a local bar to play darts and chat. She wasn't forthcoming about her new job—she'd confessed to quitting the coffee shop and taking a nanny gig but gave no details. Her friends were trustworthy, but she didn't want to spend the evening answering questions about Asher Lowe.

Maddy crept up the stairs, finding her way in the darkness to Ella's room. She pushed the door open silently, her gaze taking in the sight on the bed: Ella curled up into Asher's shirtless, jean-clad body, burrowed into his warmth. She moved into the room, wrinkling her nose at the faint sour smell. Was that vomit?

Moving to the side of the bed, she stared down at Asher and then bent over, sniffing him. She pulled back slightly, her gaze traveling up his heavily muscled chest with its light furring of brown hair, up the column of his neck, lingering on his strong jaw line and perfectly shaped lips, examining those enviable cheekbones…she gasped.

His eyes were wide open, staring intently.

She drew herself up and moved back as he sat up, careful not to disturb Ella.

He gestured toward the door and Maddy tiptoed out of the room. He followed, pulling the door shut behind him.

"Are you sick?" she whispered.

"No." He turned toward his room.

She reached out to stop him, her fingers barely skimming his bare back. His smooth skin radiated heat. He flinched and she pulled her hand away. He spun back to face her, and she wasn't familiar with the expression on his face but it looked pained.

"Is Ella okay?"

He nodded.

"Asher, were you drinking?"

He made a low sound, between a grunt and a groan, and didn't meet her eyes. "No. I haven't been drinking. Yes, Ella threw up. Too much cola, too fast."

She groaned inwardly. Really? She was pretty sure "soda" hadn't been on the list she'd left for him. For a smart guy, he was hitting some low notes in the parenting department.

"She's fine. I promise."

Her eyes narrowed.

He was hiding something and refusing to make eye contact.

She stepped closer, worried, and he finally raised his head, giving her a glimpse of the hot longing in his eyes. She froze. An answering heat swept through her, triggering a wave of dizziness.

He grunted and moved toward her, closing the gap in one stride.

Maddy stood rooted to the ground.

He yanked her into his arms with a growl and lowered his head. Leaning in, he licked his way inside her mouth, devouring her.

Maddy had been kissed plenty. But this was more than a kiss. This was conflagration. His lips and tongue were hotly demanding, and she answered his need with her own. She moaned, a sound of lust mingled with frustration, muffled by his mouth. His grip on her hips tightened and she became aware of his raging erection as it pressed, almost painfully, against her belly. She squirmed, one hand threading through the thick, satiny hair at his nape, the other pressing against his hips, wild to get closer.

It took her a few seconds to realize he was pulling away, pulling her from him. Shame washed through her, heating her cheeks. What had she done?

He backed up two steps, hands up, palms facing her. "I'm sorry, Maddy. That was totally inappropriate. I promise it won't happen again." He took another step back. Maddy held a hand to her forehead, body rigid with humiliation. He'd practically had to peel her off of him. *God.*

"No, *I'm* sorry. I…I—"

"Let's just forget it, okay? It's late; we're tired."

"Okay," Maddy whispered. She stood, frozen in the middle of the hallway, until his retreating back disappeared into his darkened bedroom.

• • •

Maddy closed her laptop after she sent her mother the e-mail with her flight information and Christmas plans. She had finished her final paper and hit the send button early this morning. Graduation was just a technicality now.

It had been a week since that kiss in the hallway. No matter how hot he was, no matter what her feelings toward him, he was her boss. The kiss, earthshaking as it was to her, was probably an imperceptible tremor to him.

She rose from the kitchen table to prepare for the trek to the bus stop to collect Ella when the sound of someone clomping down the stairs drew her attention. He'd been home a lot more lately, in his study most of the day, on the phone or in virtual meetings. Apparently, there was a lot more to being a successful rocker than just showing up for recording sessions and tours.

"Asher."

"Hey, Maddy, I thought I'd pick up Ella." He fixed an assessing gaze on her.

She was getting used to his intense looks. Unfortunately, her feelings for him were not limited to sexual interest. She loved watching his interplay with Ella. Even the therapist had told Maddy this week that she'd noticed a perceptible change in their relationship.

She'd had a chance to meet some of the band members and management team now that Asher was working from home more. She had seen his charming manipulations as he conducted business a handful of times. This megastar Asher was nothing like the Asher she knew. Rock god Asher never lost his cool, even when the fine lines of tension around his mouth illuminated his stress like a beacon. It disturbed her on some level that she could read him so well, but what was more disturbing was the inner turmoil he created in her. Living with him since that kiss created a dizzying mixture of lust and compassion. Straight lust would be so much easier to squelch.

Maybe that was what Justin had been warning her about. Not the arrogant, charming manipulative cad Asher was in public, but the oddly vulnerable, fascinating man he was in private. If so, she was in deep trouble. It was no longer so easy to dismiss him as a shallow playboy. This Christmas break away from him would be good for her, though she dreaded the time away from Ella.

"Okay. I wanted to let you know about my travel plans…" she trailed off at the look on his face and bit her lip. His expression seemed lost, somehow. It would be lonely for him and Ella without Dee, and sharing the holiday with Sterling was out of the question.

"Can you walk with me? I'd rather not discuss it around Ella," he replied, looking away.

"Sure."

She preceded him through the door and down the steps. They walked down the long circular driveway and Asher entered the gate code.

"I have plans to be gone for eight days."

Asher sighed.

"I'll leave the day before Christmas Eve, and be back two days after New Year's." She met his eyes and twisted a strand of hair. "I'd hate for Emma to have a setback. Promise you'll call if she needs me?"

"Her therapist seems to think she can handle it. That reminds me, I upgraded your phone."

Maddy stopped walking, hands on her hips. "Damn it, Asher."

He stopped and turned around, then held up a hand at the

expression on her face.

"Your cell is ancient. I got you a phone like mine so Ella can see you while you're away."

Oh. As long as it was for Ella's sake. Still, the car, the phone. What was next? It was uncomfortable having your life upgraded by the employer you had the hots for. "I wish you'd just talk to me about this stuff. My mom has a computer we could use."

"This is easier. We can use our phones."

Reaching out he gave her hand a tug. "It's just communication, Maddy."

"It's just another expense, Asher."

He studied the sky, deliberately ignoring her.

"I know you don't get it, Mr. I-have-a-gazillion-dollars, but all these expenses add up, and it's not necessary."

"It is."

"And I'll have that plan long after you guys don't need me anymore."

But she didn't even want to think about that. Living with them was fulfilling needs she wasn't even aware she had. That ridiculous mansion even seemed like home now, but long term?

"Asher—"

"Can you please just stop worrying about the money? It's getting old."

"I'm sorry if my relative poverty makes you uncomfortable. I was raised by a single mother in a small town. I learned early in life to be conservative with money, Asher. This isn't something I can switch on and off. It's who I am."

"You should have told me you were booking a flight. I could easily send you in the jet."

"Are you even listening to me?"

"I'm tuning you out," he replied.

Two rapid steps took her around and in front of him, and he walked into her upraised arm. "Damn it. This is what I'm talking about! Between scheduling my doctor appointments, getting me a car, a new phone…even my own mother is not this controlling! You need to stop doing this stuff without checking with me. I moved three thousand miles to get away from one overprotective person. I don't need you as a replacement."

He scoffed at this. "You're stubborn, unreasonable, and miserly to a fault."

What an asshole! This from the son of a billionaire who had never known a moment's concern about bills or loans or any of it.

"Go on, Asher, tell me how you really feel!"

He walked around her arm.

She wrapped her arms around herself, stomach twisted into a knot. Should she go back to the house? Screw that. Putting her shoulders back, she continued on to the bus stop, a few steps behind him.

Once they arrived, Asher stood next to her arms folded across his chest.

She avoided his glances, her body stiff.

"Maddy, I'm sorry, but you push every button with that 'silver spoon' crap. I grew up with money and affluence, so, yeah, I've had more than my share of advantages, a great education, and a last name that opens doors. But I've been on my own since I turned eighteen. I've never taken a penny of his money and I never will."

She turned to face him. "Oh."

"Being *his* son has been equal parts handicap and asset in my life."

"I'm sorry. I didn't know."

He put an arm around her shoulders and pulled her toward him, giving her a brief hug. She cudgeled her body's traitorous reaction to his heat, his casual touch.

One long, callused finger trailed down her cheek, lingered under her chin and lifted it, forcing her gaze to meet his. "I'm sorry," he said, again. "I'll check with you, okay? But can you try not to be so high handed?"

"That's the pot calling the kettle black!"

He laughed, perfect white teeth flashing.

She tried to calm her racing heart.

"I'll try, Maddy, but I've had a lifetime of getting my way."

Chapter 10

Screaming woke Asher from a dead sleep in the wee hours of the morning. He stumbled out of bed in his boxer briefs and was half-way to the door before the origin of the horrible noise registered.

My God. Ella.

He hit the hallway at a dead run and burst into Ella's room. It took him a second to find her amid masses of pink and blue pillows and what must've been fifty stuffed animals. He gathered her shrieking figure into his arms. The therapist warned him he might be in for a few rough nights as she adjusted to Maddy's absence.

He switched on the bedside lamp and dug her blanket out from beneath the covers, offering it to her. Scooting back, he positioned himself against the headboard. Sadie, the cat, hopped up on the bed and curled herself into a ball.

Ella lay sobbing in his arms, trying to find comfort with her thumb, but the tears made it impossible. Her eyes glittered in the dark room. She finally fitted her thumb in, her body jerking against his with the occasional hiccough. After a few minutes she tilted her head back to gaze up at him. "Why did Maddy leave me?"

"Christmas is coming, sweetie, and she has her own family."

"But I want her."

"I know, honey but she has a mommy who misses her and friends—"

"Does my mommy miss me?"

Asher's gut churned, a hollow emptiness in his core. Every time this kid asked about Dee it was some question he didn't know how to answer.

"What does Maddy tell you when you ask that question?"

"She tells me my mommy is watching over me so she doesn't miss me, but I can't see her so I miss her."

Sounded reasonable. "Well, that's right."

"Is Maddy watching over me?"

"No. She's in Virginia, not…not dead."

"Will she come back?"

"Yes, honey, she'll come back to us."

"Tomorrow?"

"Uh…no."

The tears started flowing again, and Asher handed her the little satin blanket.

"She's never coming back to me, is she?" Ella said around her thumb.

"She is, Ella. I promise."

"When?"

"In a few days."

"Can I see her?"

"Sure, we'll FaceTime with her in the morning."

"Is it morning now?"

He checked the clock on the dresser. "Honey, she's still sleeping."

"Please?"

"I don't want to wake her. In a few hours, we'll call her on my phone where we can see her too, okay?"

He settled her back against the pillow and rolled out of the bed.

"Uncle Asher?"

"Yes?"

Solemn, brown, tired eyes looked up into his. "Are you going to leave me, too?"

The hollow pit in his stomach burgeoned.

God.

"No, Ella. I'll always be here for you," he choked out.

But despite a call to Maddy the next morning and Asher's best efforts to wear Ella out with a trip to the beach, the same scenario repeated itself the next night.

The next afternoon, he sat on the couch with his laptop, eavesdropping on Ella's play with her ponies. Sure enough, the animals were enacting concerns about the missing Maddy.

Asher put his laptop down and went into the next room to call the therapist.

The woman sighed. "Yes. We discussed this possibility. She's bonded with Maddy and she's afraid of losing her. It's normal."

"What can I do?"

"Not much, I'm afraid."

"Then what's the best thing at this point?" he asked.

"Well, obviously the best thing for Ella would be for Maddy to come back, but—"

"I can't do that to her. She has Christmas plans—"

"—or for you to go to her."

He hadn't considered that. He stared at the tree with all the presents Justin had wrapped lying under it. Pack all that up and fly to DC? He smiled. "I'll give her a call." Moments later he dialed Maddy's cell phone.

"Asher? How's Ella?"

"Up the last two nights, having some trouble. Therapist thinks—"

"I'll come back. Can you get me a flight today?"

"How about we come to you?"

There was a long pause.

"Oh. Okay."

"We can rent a house."

She laughed. "Asher, I live in Podunk. There aren't houses for rent here and the only motel is a dump. You'll stay with us."

"Oh, no. We couldn't do that."

"My mom will insist. I insist."

"Really, Maddy, I don't think—"

"Asher, please, there's a spare bedroom and Maddy can bunk with me."

He ignored the traitorous leap in his chest.

"Well, just…check with her, okay?"

"Don't need to. She'll be thrilled."

"Okay. We'll be there later today. I'll arrange the flight."

He hung up the phone as Justin walked in. "Asher, I'm headed out in a few hours. Any last minute stuff you need?"

Asher grinned. "As a matter of fact, there is."

• • •

"Let's go out for breakfast." Asher rubbed his hands together and playfully winked at Maddy. She looked good in her mother's cheerful kitchen. Relaxed and happy. He was glad to be here and Ella was beyond excited. It was the right thing.

"Yeah!" Ella answered.

Maddy leaned against the kitchen counter. Her mother waved her hands. "Not me, I have too much to do this morning."

"Please, Mrs. Anderson." Ella begged.

Maddy's mom laughed. "No, little monkey," she replied. "I'll see you when you get home and we'll play Candyland with candy, okay?"

Ella squealed.

There were only two breakfast places in town, so Maddy directed him to her favorite. Asher glanced around the place.

Spade had eaten a lot of meals in small town diners like this one when they were starting out and touring in a bus.

He glanced up as a weathered bottle-blonde approached the table. She made eye contact and smiled coquettishly.

"Incoming," he whispered.

He never expected the expression of loathing that crossed her face, quickly masked by a polite smile.

What have we here?

"Kimberly Klaus, Asher and Ella Lowe," Maddy said, tonelessly.

The woman slid into the booth next to Maddy, across from Asher and extended her hand to him with barely a glance in Maddy's direction.

"Pleased to meet you both, and welcome to Pembrook," Kimberly drawled, showing all of her perfect white teeth to Asher.

Ella went back to her coloring.

"Coffee, Deirdre," Kimberly called over to the woman behind the counter.

"I understand congratulations are in order," Maddy said, softly.

Kimberly glanced at Maddy, her cold eyes assessing, finally coming to rest on Maddy's hand gripping her coffee cup. The woman wrinkled her nose and her mouth turned down in distaste.

Asher clenched his hand into a fist under the table. What a bitch.

Maddy straightened her spine and turned her attention to Ella's drawing.

"Thanks," the woman replied, her attention already back on Asher.

"For?" Asher asked idly, taking a sip of his coffee.

Maddy gave a little negative shake of her head and ducked her head to hide a smile.

"I just got married," the woman said, breezily.

"Congratulations," Asher said. "Now," he said, leaning toward her. "Get your bony ass out of my booth," he whispered, expression deadly.

Kimberly reared back, hand to her throat, already scooting out off the cushion with her purse clutched to her side. With a glare at a dumbfounded Maddy, she flounced down the aisle and out of the diner.

Deirdre came over, orthopedic shoes squeaking as she walked. "Whatever you're having, it's on the house." She winked at Asher, pen hovering over her pad. "I don't know what you said, mister, but we're always glad to see the back of that one. Good to have you home, Maddy. You know your momma likes to make sure you're takin' good care of yourself."

The two women exchanged smiles.

Ella glanced at the adults from her study of the laminated menu. "I like this restaurant," she confided. "It's got crayons, coloring pages and a menu with pictures."

Deirdre nodded. "Thank you, little lady. What'll ya have?"

Ella turned to Asher once the waitress walked away.

"Was that a mean woman?"

Asher frowned. "No honey, she seems like a perfectly nice woman."

Maddy merely lifted her shoulders and deliberately widened her eyes.

"Not the waitress, Uncle Asher, the woman who sat next to Maddy."

Ah, his niece saw more than he thought.

"She is a mean woman, and I don't want her sour face interfering with my breakfast and giving me indigestion."

"Oh," Ella considered this. "What's ingestion?"

"An upset stomach."

"Can people make your tummy upset?" Ella queried.

Maddy responded with a heartfelt affirmative.

Ella went back to her picture.

Asher sized up Maddy, who met his gaze evenly.

"Queen of the mean girls," Maddy stated.

Ella's crayon stilled.

"New husband?"

"Everyone likes the first Mrs. Klaus," she replied, nodding at Deirdre. "Case in point."

Ella seemed completely disinterested in the adult conversation, but he noticed Maddy was keeping a watchful eye.

Maddy gave him a small smile. "I don't approve, you know."

Asher gave her his best innocent expression.

"Word travels fast in a small town," she warned.

"So?" He shrugged, picking up his mug. "People will give me a wide berth."

She almost spit out her coffee. "Ha! You wish. That wasn't what I meant. Handing Kimberly her walking papers? She'll blab to whoever will listen. They're probably building a statue of you in the square as we speak."

"It's that bad?"

"It's only been a few months, but Kimberly is definitely the villain."

"Not Mr. Klaus?" he asked.

"Most people just think there's no fool like an old fool and give him a pass."

"What's your issue with the Queen of Mean?"

Ella's gaze came up from her coloring, hopeful.

"It's just an expression, sweetie, there's no queen," Maddy confessed.

Ella went back to her drawing.

"I don't want to get into it," she stated firmly, meeting Asher's gaze directly.

His eyes dropped to her scarred hands.

Her expression turned rueful. "Yeah, not so nice about these." She shook her hands. "Character building," she stated. "Besides, most people were incredibly supportive and kind."

"But not your peers, led by *that*."

"There were some tough times, but that was long ago."

He could tell she was downplaying the bullying she'd been subjected to because of her rheumatoid arthritis. The idea of her being taunted while in pain made his stomach churn. He forced himself to relax his fists.

Chapter 11

"Damn, this place is a pain in the ass to get to," Shane complained, rubbing his freezing hands together and stepping over the threshold with a shiver.

"Come on in," Asher responded drily.

"Seriously man, three connecting flights, the ride from hell over a mountain pass in a crappy rental. It was harrowing, I tell you. Still, it beats going back to L.A. for the holidays and being holed up avoiding the paparazzi. Got any Scotch?"

Ella came running to the door and enveloped Shane in a hug.

"Hey, sweetheart!" Shane was good with kids—probably from all the time he spent in that boy band ten years ago. Playing to tweens and younger must have taught him a thing or two about interacting with the Nickelodeon set. It hadn't escaped his notice that Ella always reacted to Shane with enthusiasm. Maybe children just gravitated toward some people. Like Maddy and her mother, Shane was a natural. It was good to have him there, no matter the circumstances.

Shane was as boy next door as Asher was bad boy rocker. Clean-cut, blond, blue-eyed, movie-star handsome with a too-perfect, too-white smile, his surfer looks masked a quick wit and a self-depreciating nature. Many people made the mistake of underestimating him over the years, to their detriment.

Shane was routinely typecast in romantic comedies before landing his breakout role. But early promotion for his blockbuster coincided with his girlfriend pictured in a tabloid in a torrid embrace with her co-star in a movie filming in Canada. Hounded by the press, he needed a place to hide out until he went back to continue the junket for his opening in a few weeks.

After the introductions to Maddy and her mother were complete, the women resumed their tea party/Christmas movie with Ella while the two men went into the kitchen.

"How are you doing?" Asher opened the fridge and chucked a beer bottle to Shane.

"Eh." Shane popped the top and took a long swallow.

"Did you know?" Asher asked.

"Let's say I suspected. She had an excuse for staying up there since they're past deadline on the film and she has almost no time off, but…"

"You've been together, what? Six months?"

Shane nodded and finished the bottle.

"Long-term for you. But you don't seem too broken up about it," Asher said.

Shane's lips twisted. "I'm not. I was into her when we started. But the separations have killed it. As usual."

"Been there. Not fun."

"Yeah. It's just the way she did it, you know?"

"Has she called?"

"Yep. That's how I had a chance to get here before all hell broke loose. Trust me, man, I'm not upset it's over, but it sucks to have it all be so public." He gave a humorless laugh.

Asher shook his head.

"I end things before they get ugly," Shane said.

"Don't we all?"

Shane nodded. "I know. Any talent in this town?" he asked hopefully.

"No. Keep it in your pants. It's a small town. The mayor came to see me this morning to ask me to perform in the Christmas pageant."

Shane's mouth dropped open. Then he bent in half, laughing. When his chuckles died down he said, "I'm envisioning your tatted up ass wrapped in a robe with a rope for a belt and a staff."

"A lowly shepherd? You wound me."

Maddy came into the kitchen and stood next to Asher. "What's up?"

"I'm recruiting for the pageant, Maddy."

Her eyes lit up. "Wonderful! He's a great actor, but can he sing?" she wondered aloud, giving Shane the once-over.

Asher choked on his laughter and Shane backed away, hands up in front of him.

"Shane thinks I've agreed to a part in the nativity play."

"Really? No, that wouldn't work. But a duet? How about 'Silent Night'?"

Shane cast a "save me" plea at Asher, who laughed. "Do you need me to get the mayor back here to ask you? We get to be in the parade, too. Maddy wants me to wear leather pants."

Shane snorted.

Maddy blushed. "Asher, it's what people expect from a rock star."

"Maddy, I'm not Elvis. I'll freeze my nuts off!"

It was Shane's turn to laugh.

"Are you really going to be in the pageant?" his friend finally asked.

"He's going to sing and play guitar. Are you musical?"

Shane grinned at Maddy. "Yeah."

"Maddy, Shane was in TruAchord."

She stared at Shane for a moment, and Asher knew the moment the light dawned. "Wow!" she said eyes alight. "I loved TruAchord when I was a kid."

Asher smirked at Shane's pained expression. "That's more enthusiasm than she mustered for Spade."

Maddy gave Asher a gentle punch in the chest. "Not true. You know I love your music."

"But you looooved TruAchord," he mimicked.

"C'mon, Asher, every teeny bopper in Virginia loved TruAchord when I was growing up. No offense," she said hurriedly, with a quick glance at Shane.

"I think it was better when she just thought of me as an actor and not a boy bander."

"So, will you?" she asked, giving Shane a searching look.

"Don't bother saying no," Asher advised. "If she doesn't wear you down, the mayor and town council will come over—"

"I'm game. Clearly I've done worse in my career."

• • •

Christmas Eve Asher rose from his seat and went to the front of the church where a guitar lay in its case next to a chair. He strapped it on and took a deep breath. This was their "Blue Christmas" and he was playing the requisite Elvis tune.

People started forward to light candle in remembrance of loved ones they wouldn't get to share the holiday with. He studied his hands, focusing on the song, not the townspeople making their way up the aisle. Halfway through the song, he saw Ella rise. She went forward with Maddy's mom to light her candle for Delilah.

The grief nearly strangled him. He stopped singing and stared down at the instrument in his hands, his fingers still automatically plucking out the chords.

Oh God. Not here. Not now.

He tried to force the waves of pain down, the way he always had before, but they kept coming. He lifted his head, his eyes searching for Maddy.

Maddy whispered something to Shane at her side, and as if in a dream he saw his friend rise from his seat, walk up to Asher and take the guitar. Without thinking, he bolted for the side door exit. Before the door shut behind him he heard Shane's baritone pick up the chorus.

It was a cold night but he didn't feel it. Didn't feel anything but the howling, raging beast of grief that would no longer be suppressed. He looked up to discover he was at the edge of a cemetery, surrounded by death.

He spotted a bench in the shadow of a huge oak tree a few feet away and picked his way through tombstones to it. Hunching over, he covered his face with his hands. God. Nothing like having a public breakdown. It could be worse—it could've been L.A.

He was so lost in his misery he didn't even hear her approach. He smelled her though, and looked up to see her standing in front of him. He dropped his gaze back to his lap.

"Maddy," his chest was so tight with the effort of holding in his rage and grief he could barely force the words out, "can you give me a minute?"

Her feet moved steps closer and her arms went around his shoulders. She yanked his head to her abdomen, her grip surprisingly strong and fierce. He gave a halfhearted struggle but ceased when her fingers resting on the top of his head slid down, massaging him from the top of his head to the base of his neck in sure, firm, strokes. Had anyone ever done this for him? His throat burned and he squeezed his eyes shut.

"Asher?" Maddy said, in hushed tones, "can you talk about it?"

He shook his head, but his hands moved from fists at his sides, to curl around her hips and hold her. Despite the love and support he got from Dee, they were never equals. He was always the big brother. The one she counted on, not the other way around. They had been everything to each other. Dee was the first person he loved.

He worried about her when she was away at boarding school, and as they got older, he was the one who arranged for them to spend holidays together. Then she went through that partying stage, and he'd been well aware that she was dancing on the edge of a cliff with a dangerous crowd. He'd been exposed to that—hell, he brushed up against it on a daily basis in his career—there were a hundred and one paths of self-destruction on the way to that cliff, and he'd learned just how close he could get without going over. Since his work ethic didn't allow for endless partying, he'd always been able to manage that aspect of the life.

The pregnancy saved her. But they were never as close after Ella came. It wasn't that Ella supplanted him in Dee's affections. It was more that he wasn't sure how to adapt to their changed status. After she gave birth to Ella, she had renewed confidence, a focus to her life, and he was too busy to cement the bond with Dee and Ella. She'd tried to bring him into her new life, but he'd floundered.

The final straw had been her forgiveness of Sterling. Asher gritted his teeth at the betrayal. If only Dee had been able to see his father for what he was. Anger welled up in him, his grief mixed with rage. His body shook.

He couldn't say a word, couldn't trust himself.

Her hand at his shoulder tightened, but her fingers moved through his hair tenderly. He could feel her embrace pulling all the despair and rage out of him until he was limp.

How long had they been out here? She must be freezing. He pushed her hips away and lifted his head to meet her gaze. Her cheeks were tearstained, her gaze full of concern.

"That damn song and those people with their damn candles," he said, with a shaky laugh.

"Yeah."

"Ready?" he asked.

Maddy shook her head and moved to sit next to him on the bench, taking his hand. Hers was freezing. He took it between his two warm ones. "We need to get you back inside. It's cold out here, it can't be good for—"

"Tell me about Dee."

He gulped and turned his head away. "Please, Maddy. I can't. Not now. I'm hanging by a thread here."

"I know, but you need to. And Ella needs to hear about her. Part of helping her through her grief is acknowledging her mother, talking about your memories."

"I can't." He turned slightly away and freed a hand to rake it through his hair, eyes downcast.

"Can you at least tell me why you were so overcome in the church?"

"Guilt."

"Guilt about what?"

Raising his head, he met her concerned gaze and suddenly he couldn't stop the words. "You name it. That she had a lonely childhood. That after she had Ella, things were awkward, our relationship changed and I wasn't sure how to handle it so I...I avoided her. But mostly because, when she died I was angry with her for having a relationship with that son of a bitch we call a dad." His voiced cracked and he covered his face with a hand, hoping Maddy couldn't see his tears.

"Do you think she understood where you were coming from?"

He groaned. "I don't know, Maddy. All I know is we weren't close and she died before I had a chance to fix it."

"But you were there for her for years, and you loved her. I'm sure she knew that."

He rubbed his lips together. "Yeah. But she wouldn't listen to me about Sterling. I all but asked her to make the choice and she kept him." God this was hard. He could barely get the words out. "She started spending holidays with him, trying to bring about our reconciliation. You have to understand, Maddy, even as a kid she always wanted to see the best in people. She got hurt a lot—I couldn't protect her from that, but I was always there to pick up the pieces. I could never understand why she let our dad into her life. And after all we'd been through, what he put us through, that was unforgivable. And you know the worst part, Maddy? I'm still angry with her. Still. And she's dead. And some days I'm so sorry I didn't have a chance to sort it out and some days I'm just furious."

He looked up, almost afraid to meet her eyes.

She had the heel of her hand pressed to her mouth, struggling to hold back sobs.

"And I'm afraid to talk to Ella. Afraid she'll see through me, see my anger and my self-disgust."

"She won't, you know," Maddy said. "She'll only see how much you loved her mom."

He stood and took her in his arms, his eyes dry and burning.

She gripped the wool covering his back and held him tightly, grounding him.

"Is that the most fucked up thing you've ever heard?" he asked, shakily.

She shook her head and leaned back to look up at him. "No. It's just really freaking sad. And I don't know what to say, only, I'm sure she loved you. It's obvious how much you loved and tried to protect her and I have no doubt that you communicated that to her while she was still alive, even if you disagreed about your father. You would have worked it out if you'd had more time."

He was silent, watching his exhalation cloud the air over her head.

A shiver shook through her.

"Maddy, you're freezing. Let's go back in."

He almost lost it again watching Ella play the role of one of the Magi. No matter how it had been explained to her, she'd insisted she was a queen and not a king. He gazed heavenward, blinking gathering moisture from his eyes, praying his sister could be aware of this moment.

Shane accompanied him on the final two songs, their voices rising and falling in perfect harmony to a traditional Christmas favorite and then a pop standard about Christmas and world peace. His gaze lit on Maddy and Ella, smiling and singing along with the crowd and managed a smile, his heart lightened.

Chapter 12

"She'll be fine, honey. More than fine. I've got her little friend, Stella, coming over for a play date and tea tomorrow," Mrs. Anderson said, giving Maddy a little push out the front door.

"Thanks, Mom," she replied. "If anything changes, let us know. Otherwise we'll see you tomorrow."

Maddy hugged her mom, then turned to give the rented Dodge a dubious look. "Asher, I dunno about this car; given the weather forecast, we may be better off taking my mom's four wheel drive," Maddy said.

"We'll be fine," Shane said, getting into the driver's seat.

"Maddy, want shotgun?" Asher asked.

"No thanks, I can direct from back here."

DC was over an hour away. What would her friends think of adding two celebrities to their night on the town? Who was she kidding—they would be all for it. It would assure them entry and VIP status at any of the clubs.

Her scene was more sports bars and casual eateries, not fancy dance places. Her friends were a different story; they were at home in the swankiest clubs. She planned to meet them in Dupont Circle, and from there, they would have dinner before going out en masse.

The trip into the city was uneventful, and Shane parked the car in an underground garage.

They entered the trendy Dupont bar. It was early—just past seven—when she spotted her two friends sitting with empty martini glasses at a large booth near the front of the bar.

Kelly and Liz sat next to each other, glancing up when Maddy walked in. The shock was unmistakable. Kelly half rose from her seat.

Both women stared at Maddy as though they'd never seen her before.

Shane laughed. "Maddy," he made a tsking noise. "You didn't tell them you were bringing friends?"

"I did," she retorted. "I just didn't tell them who."

Asher grinned and made his way to the table.

Both girls rose, star-struck.

The men offered hands and introductions. Kelly and Liz stammered their replies before they turned twin accusing glares on Maddy.

She shrugged and smiled. "Asher's my boss."

Asher rolled his eyes. "Can I get you ladies anything?" he asked, eyeing their drinks.

They told him what they were drinking, and he went up to the bar. Shane pulled up a chair and sat at the end of the booth.

Liz grabbed Maddy's arm. "Missy, you have some 'splainin to do!"

"Okay, in a minute," she said with a laugh. But first, she needed to join Asher at the bar. "Not going to take my drink order?" she asked, with feigned petulance.

He glanced over his shoulder with a grin. "I know what you drink, sweetheart. Shane too."

Maddy squelched the thrill that ran through her at his casual endearment.

The bartender came over and did a double take. "Asher Lowe!"

Asher shook his hand, put in his order and the guy started on the drinks, sneaking glances between Asher and Shane.

He put the five drinks on the bar and pointed to Shane. "That guy looks familiar…"

Maddy answered for him. "He was in TruAchord."

"Don't know them. They open for Spade?" he asked Asher.

Asher choked on his first sip of the vodka tonic. "Hell no, man. That was a boy band ten years ago."

At the horrified expression on the bartender's face, Maddy jumped in, "But he's an actor now. I'm sure you've seen him in something."

The guy narrowed his eyes. "Yeah, some action movie that's coming out soon, right?"

They nodded and Asher gathered up three of the drinks, Maddy the other two.

Before they even arrived back at their table, Maddy noticed the bartender furiously texting.

Shane had Kelly and Liz eating out of his hand. She slid into the booth next to Asher and gave each of her friends a little kick under the table. They reluctantly pulled their attention from Shane.

"I can't believe you," Kelly said. "Why wouldn't you tell us?"

"It's not her fault, it's mine. I'm kind of a nut about privacy, at least I have been since my sister died." Maddy squeezed his knee under the table.

Asher grabbed it, holding it atop his rock-hard thigh.

She felt a wave of heat sweep through her body. She'd meant to give reassurance, but the thick, warm muscles underneath his cotton pants triggered lust. She gave herself a mental shake and tried to withdraw her hand from his calloused palm, but he didn't release it. She wiggled it, he squeezed back, then flipped it palm-down, holding it atop his thigh, and with the heavy weight of his hand kept it there.

Afraid to move, dizzy with lust, unable to even look at him, she kept her unfocused gaze on Kelly—anywhere but on him. Maddy could feel him observing her and she prayed the bar was dark enough to hide her flushed skin, her shallow breaths.

She had completely lost track of the conversation.

Asher shrugged in response to something and he was so close that the upper half of his body moved against her. "Yeah, well, Maddy has been a godsend in helping me care for my niece, Ella."

Maddy tried to inch her hand out from under his. He shifted, and her hand slid along the light-weight cotton, dangerously close to the inside of his thigh. She froze, heartbeat thundering in her ears, awash in a riot of lust, her legs clenched together in an attempt to tamp down the aching pulsation between her thighs.

Liz eyed them curiously and continued, "Yeah. Maddy has always been like the pied piper with children." What were they even talking about? The pied piper? *Focus, Maddy.*

"Yeah, she has this immediate rapport with kids. Shane's that way, too," Asher finally spoke, but his voice was gravelly.

"Not just with the kids," Shane interjected.

Liz and Kelly turned to him as he launched into an anecdote about his run-ins with moms on the make at TruAchord shows.

Maddy sneaked a glance through her hair at Asher, who was watching her, jaw set.

She squirmed in her seat. What if she just slipped under the table? She imagined kneeling on the tile floor, sticky with alcohol, raising her arms to pull his hips forward to the edge of the seat, unzipping the fly of his pants. Her hand tightened involuntarily.

He grunted, shifting his body so the tips of her fingers came into contact with the thick, ridged mass of aroused flesh constrained against his thigh.

Shane was saying something, but only Liz and Kelly were paying any attention.

His palm was loose atop the back of her hand. Waiting.

Pulse pounding, her hand moved incrementally to cover his throbbing erection, her eyes widening as her fingers explored the length and girth of him.

He let out a sound—a gasp.

Maddy's fingers clenched in reaction and Shane's head whipped toward him.

"Dude?"

Maddy snatched her hand back and grabbed her drink off the table, finishing it in three desperate gulps.

Oh my God. Oh my God.

Shane stared at Asher. Then at the flood of people entering the bar. "Asher? Didn't you tip the guy?"

Asher's expression turned sheepish and Maddy snuck a glance at him. She didn't think she'd ever seen that particular look cross his face.

"Nah. "

Shane shook his head sadly. "Dude."

"Tip him?" she asked confused. "Asher, I'm pretty sure you tipped him generously."

"Not that kind of tip, Maddy." Shane responded. "Money to keep our visit on the down low."

The word the bartender put out meant the place was full. It wasn't just full, it was full of people gawking and crowding, which precluded any kind of privacy.

Uncomfortable, Maddy said, "Uh…I'm sorry about this. Maybe we should go somewhere else?"

"Shane and I have been here often enough to know of a few places to have a relatively private dinner." Asher began checking listings on his phone.

"That old-style place in Georgetown?" Shane asked.

Asher nodded and looked at the girls in askance. "American food okay with everyone?"

Of course they'd agree. Maddy was pretty sure they'd agree to eating at the falafel truck outside to keep the evening going. As they made their way out to the cab at the curb, Liz and Kelly continued to marvel at how fast the word spread. It was the only bar on the block with a line at eight P.M.

Shane got in the front, Liz and Kelly scrambled across the back, and Asher held Maddy back. Once the girls were seated he got in, folding his long body, still holding Maddy's hand. Wordlessly he pulled her in. It was a tight fit, and Maddy ended up half sitting on Asher in the back. She struggled to get comfortable on his leg, holding herself up with one arm on the back of the bench seat, trying to minimize contact with his body.

He reached up with his hand, draped her arm around his neck and settled her onto his lap. She moved, inadvertently grinding her bottom into Asher's hard thighs. He held her down with a heavy arm across her hips and whispered harshly in her ear, "Stop wiggling."

While Liz and Kelly chatted with Shane, Maddy tried to pretend she was anywhere but where she was, sitting on Asher's lap. She closed her eyes. That didn't help. He smelled divine. She could never figure out if it was cologne or bath soap or just his smell—leather combined with something vaguely citrusy—but it wreaked havoc with her libido. Tingling heat washed through her, turning her limbs into a slushy jumble. She pressed into his big, warm body as her heart rate tripled.

Asher's hand across her thighs tightened, his long fingers playing at the hem of her dress, lightly resting against the silky material covering her thighs, their tips barely touching her bare flesh.

Her face was just inches from his as she fought the temptation to rest her head on his shoulder. She shivered at the press of his huge, warm palm at her thigh. The motion of the cab as they made their way across town bumped her body against his and lulled her into relaxing further into him. She opened her eyes.

Hot, unblinking hazel eyes bored into her until she drew in a shuddering inhalation. His gaze dropped to her lips, which parted on a sigh. The large hand on her thigh pressed her down against him, using her hips to stroke his lap, his erection prodding the curvature where her thighs met her ass. Kelly was pointing out the window at various nightspots along the route, suggesting places for post-dinner dancing.

Maddy shifted so she was seated on his lap, directly over him, leaning forward, she gripped the seat back in front of her. Her coat covered his hands, which slid beneath the wool, bunching up her dress and stroking up to her thighs, then clamping down on her hips in an iron grip. He rocked her against himself, taking advantage of the combination of lousy suspension and potholes to grind her more tightly against him with every bump. She squirmed and closed her eyes, willing one of his hands to venture down to the apex between her thighs.

She felt someone's gaze on her and opened her eyes to find Shane turned in his seat, staring at them. He winked before turning back to Liz and Kelly, who were regaling him with tales of their misspent college days at bars along the route.

The driver let them out in front of an old, large, two-story brick building, a mansion in this part of town. Maddy exited the cab on shaky legs with a little help from Shane.

Asher stayed behind to pay the fare so Shane held the heavy wooden door while the group trooped inside. They all knew the place since they'd gone to college nearby, but it was so far outside Maddy's price range, she'd never eaten there.

The maître d' was an impeccably dressed older gentleman who asked for their reservation. Smiling, Asher told him they didn't have one.

"Party of five, private," Shane stated, moving forward and pressing a bill into the man's hand. The man shrugged, studied his leather-bound book on the podium, and pursed his lips. He excused himself and headed through the dining room where he was stopped by a formally dressed waiter who had been eyeing their group, Shane in particular. The young waiter whispered in the old man's ear, and the maître d' came back immediately, face wreathed in smiles, to pick up five menus and ask them to follow.

"Should we wait for Asher?"

Shane cast a knowing look at Maddy. She felt the heat rise in her face and gave a tiny shake of her head.

"I'm sure he'll be along." Shane said with a wicked grin.

The man led them to a back dining room on the first floor. It was a cozy spot with European style, historical prints on the walls, silk-shaded brass oil lamps on tables and best of all, fires crackling in several fireplaces, giving it a warm, romantic feel. Their club attire didn't mesh perfectly with the dress code in the traditional restaurant, but no one was asked to put on a jacket and tie either.

The perks of celebrity.

Asher finally joined them after their drink orders had been taken. He'd barely settled into his chair when he reached into his pocket for his phone. He answered it with a puzzled air.

"Oh, good. Yeah, we're having dinner." He gave Maddy a nod and smile across the table and she relaxed. Nothing bad, then.

"That's not good. No, we won't attempt it. We'll make plans to stay here. I wasn't wild about the drive late at night anyway. No problem. Hey, thanks again."

He put the phone away and looked at Maddy first and then Shane. "Your mom says they're already getting some freezing rain tonight; in the higher elevations it could ice up and she's worried about the roads. I told her we'd stay in town."

Maddy sat back in her chair. "Is Ella all right?"

"Great."

"Okay then. Should we book a room?" All eyes turned to her and the heat rose in her face. "I…I meant *rooms*."

"I'll take care of it after dinner," Asher answered, studying the menu.

He'll take care of it? Oh God. And he wasn't making eye contact. What did that mean? Did he think she wanted to share a room with him? Did he want to? Did he think she wanted to continue what had happened in the bar? In the cab? Who even instigated any of that?

She picked up her lemon drop martini with a trembling hand. If ever there was a situation that called for alcohol, this was it.

With the car left in a parking garage and no plans to go back tonight, both men ordered another round and discussed clubbing options with Liz and Kelly.

By the time they left for the club Kelly suggested after dinner, the three drinks had muted Maddy's anxiety. Pleasantly buzzing, Maddy climbed into the cab—this one a minivan that didn't require lap dancing.

There were no pretentions to the venue selected. No VIP areas. Just great DJs and dancing. Shane showed off some of his TruAchord moves, which had them in stitches trying to follow him.

A slow song came on and Asher swept Maddy up in his arms. She melted into him, shifting her body weight to and fro, her body automatically following the rhythm of his.

"Maddy?"

She looked up and lost her step at the intensity in his eyes. He lowered his head slowly.

Her hands, which had been resting on his shoulders, crept around to his neck, then to his head, bringing him to her. She threaded her fingers through his thick hair and urged him to her lips. Their mouths met, tongues tangling.

His body, taut with tension, pressed against her as his large warm hands swept down her body, lingering on her hips, tugging them against him.

One of her hands strayed to his back and his hips, finding its way under his shirt to the damp, hard flesh.

Asher's hands fused her body to his and she laid her head on his chest. The slow song had changed to one with an upbeat tempo, but they shifted in a slow circle, drifting as one in a crowd of whirling limbs and strobe lights.

"Let's go," he whispered.

Maddy nodded.

• • •

Maddy was as jacked up as if she'd had a triple shot at the coffee shop. Heart racing and mildly nauseated, her body radiated tension as Asher slid the white key card into the slot of the door at the Four Seasons suite. If only she'd had more to drink and she could shut off the voices shrieking "stay" one moment and "bail" the next. God help her, she was nearly coming out of her skin. This would be a mistake of cataclysmic proportions.

She'd seen the kind of women he dated—twelves on a scale of ten. He was her boss. But none of that mattered. She was in the hotel suite with Asher tonight.

What are you doing?

The rigid control she kept on her feelings for him had been completely overwhelmed in the cemetery of the old Pembrook church. God knew she'd never been immune to his attractiveness, but living with him revealed so many appealing facets of his character.

Each time she glimpsed his mouth, every time she got close enough to smell his citrusy leather scent, her body quickened. Her feelings for him were much more complicated than lust. Lust she could deny. Her heart ached for him.

"I want you," he admitted baldly. "More than I've ever wanted anything in my life."

She stepped closer to him, trembling.

He moved closer to her and yanked her into his arms, holding her up against him. His chest rose and fell. She stared into his eyes, hot and heavy-lidded with desire. His face was serious, intent, tense. Then his lips met hers and she stopped thinking at all.

Maddy reveled in his hard lips on hers. His kiss tasted of urgency—the desperation of passion long denied.

She moaned her pleasure as her tongue met the slick, wet, thrust of his. Asher's hands came up behind her head, locking her mouth to his, feeding at her, spiraling out of control.

She whimpered as his mouth left hers to explore her face, the sensitive areas on her neck, stroking, teasing, and leaving a burning trail of sensation. Her pulse accelerated as his tongue laved the thick coursing of blood in the veins of her neck. His body bowed with tension, pressed against her knees to chest, his hands swept down her body, binding her hips tightly, urgently against his.

Her hands left his hair and drifted down to the muscles in his shoulders, the ridges of his abdomen. She unbuttoned his shirt and slid her mouth away from his, panting. Laying her cheek against his warm, hard chest, she listened to his thundering heart in wonder. She gave his nipple an open-mouthed kiss, then a tiny nip.

His body shuddered in her arms. His hands yanked her hips harder against the swelling in the front of his trousers. Pulling the heavy cotton dress shirt out of his pants, she savored the feel of his hot, bare flesh where it met his waistband. She traced the seam covering the zipper of his pants. His hand fisted in her hair as she explored his thickness, the outline of his throbbing hardness. She stroked him, once, ungently, and he made an anguished sound, pulling his hips away, giving her more room to caress him. Her hands shook with desire and nerves.

He pushed her back until she was sitting on the edge of the bed, but instead of joining her, he disappeared into the bathroom, emerging moments later with a foil wrapped condom.

Wordlessly she raised her arms and he strode across the room, roughly yanking her dress up and off, leaving her clad only in her lacy panties and bra. He unhooked the clasp, stroking the sides of her breasts as he removed it. She shivered, nipples tightening into peaks of arousal. He met her eyes as his fingers caressed the tip of one nipple. She closed her eyes and moaned. It was indescribable. The ache of desire transmuted into an insistent pulse.

He shrugged off his shirt and pushed off his boxer briefs and pants in one swift motion. She opened her eyes to a hungry, aroused, naked man. His body was extraordinary—broad, strong shoulders; chest, shoulders, and arms covered with tattoos; a tapered waist; narrow hips; rock-hard abdominal muscles that she followed with her hand until she reached his thick, jutting cock. She wrapped both hands around it, exploring, watching in awe as his face flushed and he groaned, surging into her hands.

He pulled back, watching her hands on him. "God, Maddy," he ground out. The feel of his hot skin, his whole naked body pressed against hers, was extraordinary. She leaned back on her elbows. He stripped off her panties with impatient hands. His heated gaze met hers as his hands slowly spread her legs. One long finger trailed up her inner thigh. She shivered and shifted restlessly as his fingers moved to her cleft where she throbbed, slick and aching.

"Asher," she pleaded. Her hand at his shoulders urged him to her, desperate. He gentled her with a deep kiss, while his long fingers stroked, coaxed—preparing her.

She reached for him and he surged in her hand.

He leaned back and she could not tear her eyes away as he rolled the condom down over his erection, then spread her thighs with gentle hands. Her body shifted restlessly on the bed.

And she arched her back, eyes riveted to his. Slowly, so slowly he pushed the broad head of his cock against her warm, wet cleft, rubbing and stroking her. She pressed down, desperate to have him inside her.

He resisted her machinations and continued the slow, inexorable press forward, entering her, stretching her, making her wild. She gasped, shutting her eyes tight. It was too much; he was too much. She rolled her hips in a desperate attempt to accommodate him. Opening her eyes, she met his fierce, hazel gaze. He froze, panting, giving her time to adjust to his size. Her hands went to his hips and she grasped them, urgently, eyes still locked as he withdrew, then started forward again as her hips rocked. He thrust all the way in. A small cry escaped her and they both froze.

He started to move, more frenzied now.

She clutched at him, at his hips, shoulders. "Please," she begged.

He kissed her, licked the inside of her mouth and groaned his pleasure into her, making her frantic as he stroked in and out of her, establishing a relentless rhythm. She raked her nails down his back, mindless and panting.

She came with a long, thin wail, swept over the edge. Boneless, half-conscious, she was vaguely aware of his final thrusts. He came with a hoarse shout, then stilled.

Slowly, she surfaced, her body delightfully sore.

He'd shifted them both to the side, so she lay on one of his arms, his free arm tucked around her hips.

She stretched, experimentally, and a twinge of pain in her hip made her rub it, wincing. She peeked up and met his gaze.

He was staring with something akin to horror.

The bottom fell out of her stomach and she knifed up in the bed, scrambling, awkwardly, joints uncooperative.

Oh God.

He followed, on his knees reaching for her. She knelt stiffly in his arms. He rested his chin on her head. Gently he helped her back down and under the covers, up against his body so she was facing him. He sighed, her body taut in his arms.

"Maddy, relax."

She shook her head, throat thick with tears.

He pulled back and looked down.

"Maddy?"

She rubbed a hand over her face.

"I'm sorry—"

"Please, Asher, your pity is more than I can stand right now," she said, hoarsely.

"*What?*"

"That look you just gave me."

His voice gentled. "Maddy, I felt you flinch and saw your face. I hurt you."

She relaxed, infinitesimally. Oh. That. She sniffed. "You didn't hurt me. *Geez.* Couldn't you tell?"

"Not during. I mean after…"

"It's nothing."

He put a finger under her chin and tipped her face to meet his eyes. "Should I have been more gentle? I completely forgot about…about your RA," he said.

She frowned. "I don't need you to treat me with kid gloves. I'm not an *invalid.*"

"Okay, okay," he soothed, his hands stroking her from the nape of her neck to her hips.

"Stop trying to calm me down."

He gave a short laugh.

"What happened tonight, was…fun and…uh…entertaining," she lied. "You don't have to worry that I'm going to freak out." His expression was unreadable.

"Good," he said shortly. "Then you won't mind if I call down and have another woman sent up for the 'entertainment'? Round two?"

Maddy's eyes widened.

He chuckled as she went from stunned to pissed in two heartbeats. He held her squirming body with gentle hands. She relaxed against him and sighed. "This was a mistake, Asher."

"No, it wasn't."

"You're my boss." She felt him nod, his chin resting on the top of her head.

"A complication. We'll figure it out."

"Figure what out?" she said.

"How to do this." He squeezed her.

"I'm not going to continue sleeping with you. This was a one-time thing." Oh, why couldn't she make herself get out of the bed? Why was she continuing to lie there, trying to memorize his face, trying to sear this night into her memory?

"That's unfortunate, because I want to," he hesitated, "be with you."

What the hell does that even mean?

"Be with?" she repeated, blankly, examining him closely—his cheekbones still ruddy from the after effects of passion.

"Yeah." He reached out a hand and stroked the hair back from her the side of her face.

"But I work for you and we live together," she sputtered.

"Yeah, that part's odd."

She moved her head on the pillow but wasn't sure if she was nodding or shaking it.

"Why?"

"What do you mean, why?"

"It never occurred to me that you'd want a…a relationship. I mean," she gestured between them, "this is one thing, this chemistry, but, well, do you *do* relationships?"

His lips twisted. "I thought you'd gotten to know me these last few months."

"I have. I just…why?"

"Why what?" he asked again, impatiently this time.

"Why do you want a relationship with me?"

"The usual reasons. I care about you. I'm attracted to you." His throat worked as he swallowed, audibly.

Was he *nervous*?

"I'm sorry, what did you say?"

"I *said*, what about you?" he repeated.

"I'm scared," she blurted.

He settled her against him, until her head was resting on his bicep. She rolled onto her back and stared at the ceiling. It was easier than looking at him.

"Of?"

"Of things not working out." She sneaked a glance. "Of getting hurt. Uh…don't you like a lot of variety? 'Cause I don't think I could accept that."

He propped his head on his hand. "You think I'm fickle," he said. "I'm not. At least, not with the people I care about. I've had long-term relationships, Maddy. I'm capable of fidelity—"

"No, I know." She bit her lip, then lifted her face to his, running a hand over his jaw. She studied her swollen, gnarled hand against the perfection of his face.

"Do you?"

"Yeah, Asher, I know who you are." Her gaze met and held his; she looked away, shocked by the intensity there. "And, yeah. I like you and God knows, I lust after you. But there's a lot more at stake than heartache if things don't work out—"

"So we're not supposed to get involved because things might not work out?"

"If Ella weren't in the picture, I would take that chance."

He stroked her nude body from chest to hip.

She shivered and caught his hot amber gaze. She arrested his hand. "Stop. When this ends, I wouldn't *just* lose you."

His long fingers played with a lock of her hair.

"We'll take it slow," he said.

"We just had sex! How's that gonna work?"

He grinned and held her against his rapidly hardening body.

• • •

The next morning he found himself reaching for her, drowsily, eyes still closed. His hand met empty space, but the sheets were still warm. Lifting his head, he looked toward the bathroom. The door was ajar, the room dark. He frowned, pushed the covers back and went in search of her. He pushed open the doors to the suite and took two steps into the room before he saw her lying on the floor, wearing his shirt from the night before.

"Maddy?" He went to his knees next to her.

She pursed her lips, attempting to disguise a smile. "Asher, put some clothes on."

"What are you doing?"

"Stretching."

"Why?"

She sat up, wincing.

Oh God. He *had* hurt her, despite her denials last night. He'd have to be more careful with her. "Jesus, Maddy—"

She scowled. "For heaven's sake, Asher. It's like this every morning. I have a hard time because my joints are stiff, so for the last time, it's not because of the *fucking!*"

He sat back on his heels.

Maddy glanced down his body, lifting wide eyes to his. "Seriously, Asher, put on your damn clothes, would you?"

"Should you talk to the doctor? I thought the drugs—"

This time her sigh was definitely more peeved than patient.

"The drugs are not some miracle cure. It's rough in the morning for most people with RA, no matter what medications they're on. I'm always going to have pain and stiffness, especially in the morning. It's the nature of the disease."

"Will a hot shower help?"

She nodded. "That was next on the agenda."

He helped her to her feet. "Do you get up every morning and lie on the floor to stretch?

Her gaze slid away and she shrugged.

His eyes narrowed. "No, you don't, do you? You do them in bed. It's painful otherwise, isn't it?"

She dipped her head.

"Then you do them in bed with me."

"I'm not going to wake you up—"

Asher reached for her and tucked her gingerly into him. "It's not going to wake me up, and if it does, too bad. If you need to stretch first thing, you do. Agreed?"

She nodded against his chest.

"Now let's go take a shower."

Chapter 13

Maddy pushed open the door to Asher's master suite, clothes spilling out of her hands. He'd offered to move her things to his bedroom, but she refused. Ella was desperate to have Uncle Asher throw her around in the pool since they'd arrived back in California this afternoon.

She wandered into the walk-in closet, a closet almost the exact size and shape as the living room in her apartment. There were elaborate wood shelving units and bureaus, and though she'd rarely seen him in anything other than jeans, concert T-shirts, and combat boots, the space was nearly filled. Everything was neatly hung and folded.

It was a bit like being in a store. Surely he didn't arrange the closet? A laugh escaped her. No, this must be the housekeeper or a stylist's doing. Asher was no slob, but he was not this organized. She laid the clothes, about seventy-five percent of her wardrobe, on the ottoman in the center of the room.

She thought she'd gotten used to Asher's level of affluence as his employee. Transitioning to girlfriend, living with him, and sharing a closet was completely surreal. Add to that the fact that he was still paying her to take care of Maddy and it made things awkward—at least for her.

Asher appeared in the doorway, a shivering, towel-wrapped Ella in his arms.

"Maddy!" the little girl exclaimed, grinning in spite of her blue lips, "I'm freezing."

Asher cocked his head. "Everything okay?"

She nodded, and held her arms out to take Ella.

He shook his head. "No, I'll pop her in the tub to warm up. You sure you're okay?"

"Yeah."

"Need anything?"

Her smile was a bit forced. "No."

He studied her. "Let me get the bath running."

"I need Ariel and Ken," Ella demanded.

Maddy's smile broadened. "Are they an item now? I'll get them."

They disappeared and Maddy retrieved the dolls from Ella's bathroom. She handed them to a naked Ella, sitting hugging her knees to her chest at the bottom of the giant tub.

When the bath was full, Asher turned off the taps. "Be right back, love, gotta change out of this wet suit."

Asher drew Maddy out of the bathroom and into the bedroom, leaving the door ajar in case Ella needed them.

He took Maddy into his arms. "What's wrong?"

"Nothing, really. I'm good."

He leaned away, eyes boring into hers.

She bit her lip and broke the contact.

"Maddy."

"It's just weird, Asher, I mean I'm your employee and I'm living with you. Like, in your room. Here in L.A., it's easy to forget who you are."

"Yeah, so?"

"Isn't that weird to you?"

He shrugged. "No."

Maddy retreated and sat on the bed, staring at her hands. In Virginia, it was easier to think of him as Asher, not Asher Lowe.

He strode to the far side of the room, dropped the towel, and peeled off the wet boardshorts.

"Asher!"

He glanced up and grinned. "Whaddya expect, Maddy? I got

hard 'cause I was holding you." He grabbed a pair of cargo shorts from the chair and stepped into them.

Maddy cast a scandalized look toward the bathroom door.

"Relax. I'm not going to try anything." He had trouble with the zipper of his pants and gave a muffled laugh.

Through the door, Ella scolded the Ken doll for some imagined infraction.

He took her hand and pulled her down to sit next to him on the bed.

Maddy stared down at their linked hands. "It's awkward."

Putting a long, callused finger under her chin, he lowered his lips and kissed her gently, so gently tears sprung into her eyes.

Her heart lurched.

Oh, God. I'm in love with him.

"What, specifically, is the problem?"

Maddy covered her face with her hands. Asher put an arm around her. She raised her head and gestured to the room with a sweep of her hand. "All this, Asher. How is this going to work? If I'm your girlfriend, how can I be your employee as well?" It came out as a wail.

He settled her across his lap and kissed her again, with more hunger. He tasted of salt and smelled of pool chemicals. Arousal burned through her, turning her limbs to pudding.

He ended the kiss on a groan and settled her next to him. "What am I?"

"What?" she asked, head spinning.

"You said it was easy to forget what I am. What's that?"

"A rock star? A *Lowe*?"

"Maddy, Dee and I grew up with tremendous affluence. Your life has been fairly normal in comparison, judging by what I saw over Christmas. Yes, I'm a Lowe—and I've told you there were advantages: I can golf, ski, play polo—both kinds—sail; the things

I have a basic proficiency at would surprise you. And the ability to do those things with the children of other rich people threw open doors of access and opportunity like you wouldn't believe. Even in my business. Add to that the fact that I've had the best education available—formal and informal, all of it—"

"Okay, Asher, it's just going to take me some time to adapt."

"I'm not done. The list of things I don't know how to do is longer. How to be part of a family, how to care for a child, how to balance life and work and a million other things. I had lousy examples. And mine aren't even the worst out there. Talk to Shane one day about what it's like to be a child star—a commodity. You know about my dad. And my mother? I don't even want to go there. She's a nightmare. *You* were raised with the only things that matter. Your mom…" His voice roughened, and he paused, taking a minute to bring himself under control. "You were luckier than me. You're still luckier than me in so many ways. The love I gave and received growing up was almost exclusively from Dee. I don't want to think about what I would've been without her. So don't give me this 'you're rich and famous' crap. Not you, Maddy."

"Maddy? Uncle A?" came a little voice. "Ken wants to know what's for dinner."

Chapter 14

Maddy had barely finished wrapping herself in a towel after her shower when there was a knock.

"Babe?"

She opened the door. Asher was standing there, looking sheepish. "Can you come out here a minute?"

Worry clouded her brain. "Is it Ella?"

"No, I'm sure she's having a ball with Justin and Scott."

With a puzzled frown, Maddy hitched up the towel. Just past Asher on the bed lay a scarlet dress and the most beautiful shoes she'd ever laid eyes on. Not high, she could never wear heels thanks to her rheumatoid arthritis, but these were perfect. Her eyes welled with tears. He'd even remembered the kind of shoes she needed.

"Asher," she said, reverently.

He put his hands up. "I'd love to take the credit, but it wasn't me. Scott and Justin picked it up."

She crossed over to the bed and ran a hand gently over the material.

"Wow."

"I'm sorry, Maddy, I hadn't even considered that you might not have something to wear to Shane's premier tonight."

Maddy studied him through narrowed eyes. "I had something okay to wear. I'm not a total pauper, Asher."

"No, I know," he said, hurriedly.

She turned back to the dress, examining its vibrant hue and clean lines. "But nothing like this. It's exquisite." Maddy ran her hands over the dress again.

Asher cleared his throat, his expression disgruntled. "I wish you looked at me like that."

She laughed.

In two steps he reached her and pushed her back toward the bed.

"No…stop! The *dress*." Maddy pulled out of his arms and walked the dress over to the closet. Turning it on the hanger, she hesitated as she caught sight of the low back.

The heat from Asher's body behind her registered just before he plucked the dress from her fingers, hung it up, and grabbed her.

She clutched at his powerful shoulders, laughing as he carried her to the bed and dropped her on it. She bounced twice, still laughing. "Caveman," she managed.

He growled and stripped off his brown Henley in one smooth motion, exposing broad shoulders, a well-defined chest, slightly furred with hair, and those tattoos. God, his tattoos. What was it about that inked-up, tanned skin that liquefied her sex?

Maddy could spend the rest of her life staring at those tattoos, outlining the edges with the tip of her tongue, licking their black and colored centers. He made short work of his well-worn jeans and boxer briefs and glanced up.

At the intensity in those beautiful eyes, the laugher died in her throat. A surge of lust spun through her and her nipples formed taut peaks under the fluffy white towel.

He put one knee on the bed and used her ankles to pull her slowly toward him. A shiver ripped through her body at his stark arousal. Would she ever lose her sense of wonder that this beautiful man wanted her?

His hands pulled apart the edges of the towel, exposing her body to his narrow-eyed gaze. He gently spread her legs at the knees, then trailed long, calloused fingers up her thighs. The temperature in the room bumped up ten degrees. She closed her eyes, embarrassed and excited at being so exposed to him in broad daylight. Heat flooded her damp skin and she squirmed.

He paused at the juncture to stroke her lightly, teasing her, before his big, warm hands trailed up her belly to cup her breasts. He leaned over and pulled one nipple into his mouth and she gasped. His mouth was so wet and warm, hands moving to press her hips into the bed. Her legs shifted restlessly as the ache became a throb of need. She threaded her fingers through the thick hair at the nape of his neck and pressed his mouth more firmly to her pebbled nipple, gasping. "Asher, please."

He raised his head from her breast and grinned wickedly.

She yanked his hair, hard. He grunted and flipped her over onto her stomach, lifting her hips until she was on all fours. She clenched her quaking thighs together but his firm grasp moved them back apart. Standing behind her, he stroked the curve of her ass, all the way down to her calves, setting off more tremors. The bed sheets captured her moan as his palms made their way up her body with deliciously long strokes, deliberately avoiding the place she needed them most.

"Asher…" Hating the desperation in her voice, warmth spread across her upper chest. Finally, one hand paused in its journey, slipping down between her thighs. He pushed two long fingers into her and she clenched around him with a muffled moan. His other hand pushed between her shoulder blades. She pressed her heated face to the soft, cool sheet, supporting herself on her forearms as he explored her, curling his fingers up into her drenched, swollen flesh. Her hands twisted in the sheets and she shifted her weight, pressing back, desperate to take him inside her aching body.

She was so close, she could feel the telltale throbbing, the weakness in her limbs. She didn't want to come like this, without him. Maddy clamped her legs together, trapping his marauding fingers, and he grunted, pulling them away. The soft sound of the condom wrapper tearing was followed by his hands, urging her thighs apart.

The fat head of his cock stroked against her slippery entrance and she pushed back again with her hips, impatient. Her body shook in earnest—excited and inflamed. Her breath caught as he pushed into her, incrementally. Her hips flexed, eager to bring him fully inside.

It was his turn to gasp as she shifted back, impatient with his tempo. His hands went to her hips to still them, but it was too late. He wasn't even halfway inside her when she came with a long, low cry.

He pumped into her, hard and fast as she convulsed around him, his rough palms stroking her ass, gripping it, riding out her tremors. Over and over he stroked into her, slick and hard, until she had no recourse but to bury her face into the mattress as she sobbed out another climax. His pace accelerated, his fingers gripped her hips, digging into the flesh over her hipbones, until he came with a low guttural sound.

Maddy collapsed, too satiated to do more than roll to her side.

Asher fell next to her and spooned up against her. He licked a spot between her shoulder blades and she shivered. "Okay?" he asked softly.

"Two orgasms and the playboy wants a critique?"

He propped his head on his elbow and pulled her tighter into the heat of his body. "You know what I'm asking."

She turned her head to meet his concerned gaze with a level one of her own. "I do. But you don't need to ask every time. Maybe you should talk to my doctor. 'Doc, tell me, can people with RA make love like regular people? Should I use bubble wrap instead of a condom so I don't injure her?'"

His lips tilted up in that half-grin that she found so unbelievably sexy. "Kink, Maddy? I like it."

Her body responded with a throb. She closed her eyes. Unbelievable. They had just finished and she was ready to go again.

She rolled onto her back. "How 'bout this? If what we do is too much or uncomfortable before, during, or after, I'll let you know. Trust me when I tell you I don't enjoy pain. Will that work? It takes something away from the magic to be asked if I'm okay every time."

A smug smile settled at the corners of his lips. "Magic?"

She rolled her eyes. "It should be. All the practice you've had."

His eyes bored into hers. "Ah, my past. That's two references to my reputation in as many minutes. You want to talk about it?"

Maddy bit her lip. She hadn't meant to tip him off to her insecurities.

"Maddy?" he repeated. There was so much tenderness in his expression.

"A smidge," she admitted.

"It's different with you."

She tensed and her stomach lurched.

He gave her a gentle shake, correctly interpreting whatever expression had registered on her face at his words. "Not bad different, fantastic different." He rolled onto his back and raised his knees. She shivered at the withdrawal of his body from hers. He sat up, leaned over her, and pulled the comforter over her, tucking it under her body.

"I'm not doing this very well, am I?" he said.

She turned her head and sneaked a glance—he was staring at the ceiling. "Nope."

"I thought I'd had every kind of relationship there was, from hook-ups to committed. I've had a few long-term monogamous things that were…satisfying." He turned his head to study her and she shifted to lie on her side. "But this—with you—is different. I'm different. It's *more*."

Her heart leapt.

He reached over and tugged her toward him.

She caught sight of the clock on the dresser. "Asher! Is that the time?" She detangled herself from his arms and the blanket and scrambled from the bed. "Hurry, we can't be late for Shane's premier."

Chapter 15

Maddy poured coffee into the travel mug and slipped on her boots. Her follow-up appointment with the doctor was in an hour and she needed to stop for gas. That early morning romp with Asher was bound to make her late. Happy, but late.

Smiling, she grabbed her keys and purse and hollered up the stairs, "See you later, baby!"

Without waiting for a reply, she let herself out the front door and hurried down the steps to her car. She started the engine, humming to herself, and flipped on the radio.

It was set to a pop station courtesy of Ella. Maddy was an alternative rock kind of girl, but whenever Ella was in the car they listened to her music, and Maddy was coming to know all the tween pop stars and their infectiously upbeat songs.

She put the car into drive and froze as she heard Shane's name mentioned by the two shock jocks while they discussed his premier at Grauman's Chinese Theater last night.

They gossiped about Shane, his latest girlfriend and the cheating, speculated about his scandalous past—he had quite a history, apparently...

Poor Shane.

The iron gates to the house were swinging open when Asher's name came up.

"And what was that with Asher Lowe at the premier?"

She stared at the radio as she inched through the gate.

"Some celebrity website said he's banging the nanny."

"Man, did you get a load of her?"

Maddy's hand left the steering wheel and went to her throat. Asher warned her. She hadn't listened. It wasn't as if they knew anything about him or her or their relationship for that matter, but hearing people discuss them…She tried to pull all the way forward to let the gates close behind her, but a long black limousine was blocking the driveway. She glowered at the limo parked in front of her, gave a halfhearted honk, and put the car in park.

Her fingers hovered by the radio knob—she really should have switched it off, but she couldn't. They tore her to shreds in minutes. Her face, not pretty; her hairstyle, not hip; her clothes— they had divergent opinions on her clothes. One loved the dress, one didn't. Her looks they rated on a ten-point scale—and she didn't even make the upper half. They compared her unfavorably to women Asher had been linked to in the past. They speculated about her weight and joked about eating disorders.

A vaguely familiar sensation twisted through the pit that was her stomach as disbelief turned to hurt, and, finally, to anger. Those assholes. They were no better than Kimberly Klaus. They may have a larger audience, but it was the same level of bullying nastiness. God, she hoped Ella didn't hear about it. Maddy bit her lip. She was not going to turn on the regular radio in the car ever again. From here on in, satellite radio that played only music.

Maddy stared out her front windshield at the automobile blocking her access to the street.

What the hell? That limo still hadn't moved.

She was going to be late. With a disgusted sigh, she tapped her horn again.

Turning off the car, she hopped out, grumbling, keys and purse in hand. Striding over to the tinted window at the rear, she tapped and it rolled down. She peered in, a polite smile firmly in place.

"Excuse me, but you're blocking the driveway and I'm—" Her voice died as she spotted the woman.

Oh my God. It was Asher's mom! It had to be. She looked older than the pictures from the internet, but remarkably well preserved. Her face was in profile as she stared ahead, the sole occupant in the rear of the vehicle.

She turned, pinning Maddy with an icy stare. Asher's eyes. But Asher's eyes had never been that cold. Maddy recoiled, her hand automatically reaching into her purse for her cell phone.

"Get in," the woman said.

Maddy peered around the inside of the car.

"I'm late for an appointment, Mrs....er..." She racked her brain. What was her name?

"It's Jacqueline. Get in."

Maddy searched her purse. Where was her phone?

"Madeline?" the woman said in a conversational tone.

Maddy raised her head and looked right into the barrel of a small pistol. She blinked.

It was so small, was that thing even real?

"Do I have to ask again?" the woman said, her voice monotone, face expressionless.

Well and truly spooked, Maddy dropped the phone into her bag. It took her shaking hands two tries to open the door. Her limbs heavy and clumsy, she slid onto the seat and closed the door. The locks went down. She shot a disbelieving look at the glass partition separating the driver from the back. The car slid away from the curb into the street.

"We need to have a little chat."

Maddy scrunched herself up, getting as close to the door and as far away from the gun as possible. All her limbs were shaking now. She sneaked a glance at the lunatic next to her.

The little pistol had disappeared.

The woman offered her hand to Maddy.

Humor her! her brain shrieked. *Stay calm.*

"What can I do for you?" Maddy extended her own unsteady hand.

The woman took Maddy's thin hand with swollen knuckles. "Ugh," she said softly in a calm, well-modulated voice.

Maddy's nostrils flared, but she left her hand in the cool, elegant grip of her lover's crazy mother until the other woman dropped it unceremoniously.

"I have rheumatoid arthritis, a chronic autoimmune disease."

Jacqueline's face didn't change, but Maddy was scrutinized by her emotionless, assessing gaze. Asher intimated that his mother was a nightmare. Silly her, she'd taken that to mean annoying, not insane.

It was difficult to believe this woman was the mother of an almost forty-year-old man. She didn't look older than fifty. Was it an excess of plastic surgery, Botox, or something more ominous that prevented her from having any expression?

Maddy couldn't tear her gaze away from those eyes. Asher's golden eyes, icily intelligent, but intense and disturbed.

"Arthritis? At your age?"

Maddy was pretty sure her eyebrows would've risen in disapproval, disbelief, or disdain, but her frozen face didn't allow for that.

"Rheumatoid arthritis. I've had it a while." Maddy's voice quavered. *Stop thinking about the gun. Buck up.*

She made a sound of disgust and Maddy's eyes widened.

God. Why hadn't she asked more about his mother? Why hadn't he warned her?

"My son is dating a diseased woman. I was hoping you just didn't photograph well."

Maddy repressed a bubble of hysterical laughter. She bit her lip hard to quash it.

"What will it take to get you out of my son's life?" Jacqueline asked, still staring.

That gun could do a pretty effective job.

"He deserves better than you. The poor boy has lived without me all his life, thanks to that conniving son of a whore Sterling. I'm his mother and I want what's best for him," she said, in that same, flat tone. "That's not you."

"Okay," Maddy agreed.

The woman narrowed her eyes.

Here goes nothing.

"People were talking about me on the radio this morning. Saying that I'm ugly."

Mrs. Lowe nodded.

"That he deserves better. He's good-looking and successful."

"Yes. Exactly." Asher's mother continued nodding like a Bobblehead.

"And I'm none of those things."

Don't overplay this, Maddy. She's not stupid.

"I don't need that in my life. Especially since we're not serious. I was going to…you know…end things." Maddy said.

The older woman still nodded, her taffy colored hair helmet-like in its immobility.

She waited, daring Maddy to break eye contact.

"Oh, you want me to do it now?"

"I think that would be best."

"Sure." Maddy gingerly pulled out her phone under Jacqueline's watchful gaze and thumbed down to Asher's number.

The phone barely rang once when his hoarse voice answered, "Maddy?"

"Hey, Asher, listen—"

"What's happened? Why is your car in the driveway? I have the police—"

"Uh…yeah. That's not necessary. Um…listen. I think this…thing we've been doing is a mistake."

There was dead silence on the other end of the phone.

"Asher?"

"Yes."

"Did you hear me?" Her voice shook.

"Yes," he said, tone wooden. "Mind telling me why you abandoned the car at the end of the driveway?"

"It's your car," she replied. She studied Asher's mother, who was staring straight ahead. Was she buying it?

"So, it's been great and all, but I'm done. This morning there were people talking about me, trashing me, and I don't need that in my life."

He sighed. "Babe. I'm sorry you had to hear that. It's all bullshit. I never listen to that crap. We talked about this."

"I know. I know. But it's not worth it, Asher."

Sell it, Maddy. She looked over at old frozen-face.

"Asher, I've had enough bullying for a lifetime, and I don't want any more of it."

"*Fuck.* I'm so sorry, sweetheart. I really am. If there were a way to protect you from—"

"Yeah, well. There isn't, is there? So, I'm…I'm done. Okay? I don't want to see you again."

"What about Ella?"

"Her either."

"*What?*"

She glanced at Asher's mother. The woman was staring at her, eyes narrowed with suspicion. Maddy's spine stiffened and irritation laced her tone. "Look. I don't want to be with you. Deal with it. You come with too much baggage. Way too much. Goodbye."

"Maddy, where are—"

She disconnected the phone and snuck a glance at the woman perched next to her.

Had she bought it? She turned to Jacqueline, who was bestowing a magnanimous look upon her. Her phone started vibrating in her hand and she tucked it back into her purse.

Okay then.

"Do you think you could you drop me at my apartment?" Maddy asked, cautiously.

Jacqueline lowered the partition and Maddy gave directions to the driver.

Fifteen silent minutes later, the car pulled up in front of her building. Maddy got out, closed the door, and stood on the sidewalk, watching as the limo drove off. When it was out of sight, she sagged in relief and collapsed onto the curb.

She checked her watch. Damn it, she missed her appointment. Still, being the victim of a kidnapping at gunpoint seemed like a pretty good excuse.

She called Asher back. It went to voice mail. He was probably canceling the police or having the car towed.

Maybe she shouldn't be standing here on the street. That woman might decide not to take her at her word.

She fished her keys out of her purse, unlocked the door to her complex and headed up the stairs to her apartment. She needed to reschedule her doctor's appointment. Then she would call Justin for a ride.

Chapter 16

Asher glared at the phone in his hand. "What the *fuck?*"

She *called* to break up with him? And she was matter of fact about it? He didn't read gossip sites, had no idea what people were saying, and couldn't care less. His stomach knotted. Just because he had years—decades, really—of dealing with all the bullshit rumors, speculation, and lies about his life didn't mean she would take it in stride.

Gut twisting, he turned on his laptop. What had he been thinking? That she would roll with the punches? Why hadn't he seen this coming? *Shit!*

He pulled up one of the most offensive celebrity gossip websites and searched on his name.

Oh no. There were pictures of him with Maddy. And comments. Endless, horrible, cruel comments. About her appearance and weight. About her intelligence.

It went on and on.

He read with dawning horror. No wonder she broke up with him. He did a general search. More nastiness, awful stuff.

Oh my God. Those fuckers! He lifted up the laptop and hurled it across the room.

Then he picked up his coffee cup and threw it. It shattered on the opposite wall. He looked around wildly for something else to throw. His phone, his fucking phone. He enjoyed throwing it. Roaring, he swept his arms across the desk, dumping papers, files and a vase full of flowers onto the floor.

Ding-dong.

Who the hell?

He stalked to the front door and threw it open so hard it bounced against the wall.

Three men and one woman stood on his stoop. Police officers. All four simultaneously backed up a step and put hands to their side arms at his threatening posture.

He stared at them, uncomprehending.

Oh yeah.

He had called the police.

"I'm sorry, officers." He steepled his hands over his mouth. "Come on in."

"Did you call the police, Mr. Lowe?" one officer asked, stepping over the threshold, glancing around.

"Yeah."

"What seems to be the problem?"

"My girlfriend took her car and left it blocking the sidewalk. I thought something might've happened to her, but she just called. Everything's fine."

Varying degrees of suspicion were evident on each and every face.

"Please, come in." Asher moved back a few steps.

The rest of the officers filed in.

The man standing closest to him stepped forward and offered his hand. "Sergeant Greene." He introduced the rest of the group.

Asher strove for calm, eyeing the officer who stepped away from the group and mumbled something into his radio clipped to his shirtfront. Asher caught the words "domestic disturbance."

Asher's eyes widened.

Domestic disturbance?

"Why don't you all come in here?" He led them into the living room.

All four officers halted just past the threshold, staring past him.

Too late, he remembered the mess in the room.

"Mr. Lowe? Why don't we step over here," the sergeant said, standing well away from him as he pointed to the area near the fireplace, an area that had escaped Asher's rage.

"So, where is your girlfriend, Mr. Lowe?" the man asked conversationally, leading him over to the couch in front of the fireplace.

"I don't know," he replied. "She left for a doctor's appointment at nine thirty. At nine forty-five the landscapers arrived to tell me the SUV was blocking the gates and they were stuck open. I went out to see…"

The sergeant was taking notes while the other officers looked around the room.

"Mind if I check out the house?" the female officer asked.

Asher raised his hands. "Be my guest. I'm the only one home."

She and the mustached police officer left the room.

"So you went out to see about the car…" the officer prodded.

"Yeah. And it was blocking the gate, unlocked, the keys and her purse gone. I was worried so I called you people."

"Didn't the emergency dispatcher keep you on the phone?"

"Yeah, but I had a call coming in from Maddy—my girlfriend—so I told the operator to hold on and took the call." He stopped, remembering.

"And?"

"And she told me she left," he gritted out, chest tight.

The officer indicated the mess across the room with his pen.

"Did you have a fight?" he asked, calmly.

"God, no!"

Did they expect to see bent golf clubs or a bloody knife?

"It's nothing like that. After I hung up, I was mad. I…I threw some shit around."

"Is this a relationship of long standing?" the officer asked, continuing to make notes on his pad.

"I guess." What did that mean?

"With the nanny?" the officer examining the mess across the room called out.

Asher and the sergeant glanced over. The man shrugged sheepishly. "It was on the radio this morning," he said, defensively.

The sergeant sighed.

"What was on the radio?" Asher asked.

"That you're dating the nanny." Finished with his examination of the disaster Asher had made of that part of the room, he walked over and stood a foot away. "Two guys on the radio were talking about the premier of that new action film and your name came up. They were talking about your date."

Asher groaned and covered his eyes. Hadn't she said she'd heard that? *God.* He imagined the radio disc jocks were even harsher than comments on the Internet.

Poor Maddy. He would fucking kill those people. Grief turned back into rage and he could feel himself flush with it.

Both men were staring.

"So the altercation with your girlfriend—"

"There was no damned 'altercation,'" Asher bit out. "I was pissed." He gestured to the broken laptop. "They were nasty about Maddy—my girlfriend. That's why she called to break up with me. Fucking *fuck.*"

"Calm down, Mr. Lowe," the sergeant said in a tone that managed to be both soothing and authoritative.

"We need to speak with her. Do you have her number?" the other officer said.

Asher gave them her cell number. "She was on her way to a doctor's appointment this morning."

The officer stepped a few feet away, took out his cell phone, and dialed.

Dialed again.

"No answer," he said, unnecessarily, putting the phone away.

"Can you try the doctor's office?" Asher suggested. "Doctor's name is Baxter, he's a rheumatologist on Camino Real. She won't pick up the call if she's in with him."

While the other officer researched the number and placed the call, the sergeant asked Asher to run through everything that transpired that morning.

Asher sighed and repeated what he knew.

"She never showed." The officer walked over to stand next to his partner and size up Asher. The other two police officers entered the room.

"No one here. No sign of a disturbance anywhere else in the house," the female officer relayed.

Asher reached into his back pocket for his cell phone. The officer backed up a step, suddenly on high alert. He reached into the other pocket. Where was his…then he saw it, across the room.

"I'd like to get my cell phone," he told them, pointing at it. All eyes followed his finger.

The woman walked over, picked it up, and brought it to him. The phone was dead, the screen cracked.

"Goddamn it." Asher shook it and pushed buttons.

"Mr. Lowe," Sergeant Greene said. "We're going to need to take you downtown with us, until we can talk to Madeline Anderson. It's routine."

Asher stared at the man, then looked at each one of the officers in turn before shaking his head. "Not gonna happen," Asher said. "If this gets out—and if I know you people, it will—it could jeopardize my custody arrangement. I get how this appears." He gestured to the room. "If you can get hold of Maddy—"

"We haven't had any luck."

Asher scowled. "Keep trying. Maddy and I will be happy to clear up any misunderstanding, but if this gets out there will be hell to pay. Taking me downtown is guaranteed to put this in the spotlight. If I have to, I'll call my lawyer. Right now I need to get my assistant, Justin Montoya, and let him know what's going on."

The officer took down the number.

The sergeant sighed. "I'm going to call my lieutenant off-radio and see how he wants to handle this. Hold up, guys." He pointed at the female officer. "Get a tow truck to get that car back into the driveway." He stepped away to mumble into the cell phone.

The house phone rang. Asher lifted an exaggerated eyebrow, asking permission to answer his own damn calls. Sergeant Greene tipped his head to indicate permission.

Asher picked it up on the third ring.

"Man, I have been calling and calling your cell. What the hell?" Justin asked.

"My cell is busted. Listen, the police are here."

"I figured," Justin said.

His eyebrows shot to his hairline. "You figured?"

"Yeah, I've got Maddy here with me—"

"*You've* got Maddy?" he parroted.

"Yeah. We'll be there in five."

• • •

"Oh my God!" Maddy rushed into the house and launched herself into Asher's arms. His arms went around her and he held her to him in an embrace so tight it bordered on painful.

She pulled back, studied him and saw the desolation in his eyes. "Oh Asher, really?" she said, pulling him against her.

He leaned down and captured her mouth—her breath—in a soul-stealing kiss.

Someone clearing their throat caught her attention, and she stepped back.

The officers were pretending not to look at them.

Asher draped an arm around her, pinning her to his side.

Justin stood grinning in the entryway, still holding Maddy's purse. "How 'bout I go move the car?" he said.

"Yeah, keys are in there." She gestured to the bag he held.

He held it out to her.

"Side pocket," Maddy said, unwilling to tear herself from Asher.

With a grimace, Justin dug around, finding them. "Be right back."

The female police officer pulled her radio to her mouth, identifying herself to dispatch. "Cancel tow truck for Lowe residence."

One of the police officers, Sergeant Greene according to his name plate, stepped forward.

Maddy regarded him, then Asher before stepping away.

His eyes were narrowed, his face flushed and his hand fisted at his side.

"Maddy, what the hell?" Asher said.

"I'd rather talk to you about this in private," she said softly, reaching for his hand.

He shook her hand off, his face settling into furious lines. "Now that the police are involved, that's not an option. You know that's not a good thing for me, Maddy, not with the Ella situation."

Yeah, it wasn't. But neither was it the time to tell him about being kidnapped at gunpoint. She didn't need the police to hear that until she knew how Asher wanted to handle her. It was his mother, after all.

"Your mother—"

Asher's body jerked as if he'd been given an electric shock.

The officer standing closest to them put his hand to his gun reflexively.

Oblivious to their tension, he moved Maddy so she was facing him. His grip was tight on her upper arms.

The female officer stepped toward them.

Maddy squirmed but met his gaze.

"Oh my God," he said hollowly, understanding dawning.

"Yeah."

"You wanna tell us what's going on?" Sergeant Greene asked. He stepped forward, pad in hand. Maddy pressed her right foot onto Asher's toes, gently, meaningfully.

He let her go, his eyes boring into hers. "I'll get them to pick her up."

"Asher, maybe not the best idea with Sterling and the Ella situation." Maddy turned to the sergeant with a forced smile. She looked back to Asher and caught his nodding agreement to her cryptic words.

"When I went to leave for the doctor's appointment, Jacqueline—that's Asher's mom—was blocking the driveway with her limo."

Sergeant Greene stopped writing.

"Apparently she wanted to meet me."

She spared Asher a glance.

Rage sketched into his expression.

"So I left the car…I was upset about some things on the radio—"

Asher made a pained sound, and two of the police officers wouldn't meet her eyes.

Great. So everyone heard those men trashing her?

"I was with her for a bit, then I called Asher. I was upset. Not making sense. I'm so sorry for the inconvenience."

She reached to squeeze the hand Asher held in a fist by his side and laced her fingers through his resistant ones.

Justin returned, keys in hand, and swiftly shut the door behind him. He tossed them back into the purse sitting on the floor in the foyer. "I secured the gate. That's the good news. The bad news is paparazzi are swarming the street; some have come on the property," he said.

Sergeant Greene shook his head, clearly uncomfortable with the events. "Excuse me a minute while I call my lieutenant again. Keep all communication off the radio."

"Oh dear," Maddy said softly. This had the makings of a real farce.

Asher reeled her back to his embrace. "Maddy," he whispered, "I'm sorry."

Heedless of their audience, they kissed again. Maddy stifled a moan as her lips met the firm pressure of his mouth. He raked his fingers through her hair, gripping her skull, holding her head firmly while he ravished her.

She pulled him closer, eager.

"Guys?" Justin called out. "Paparazzi. On the property."

Maddy resurfaced, lethargic, lost in Asher's hot, hazel, heavy-lidded eyes.

"Mmmm?" she said absently, resting her hands on his hips.

• • •

Asher pulled away from Maddy, taking a few seconds to get himself under control and his brain reset.

"So she's fine, everything is fine. Just a misunderstanding," Asher told the three police officers in his foyer. He looked meaningfully at Sergeant Greene, who was still in a deep phone conversation, and indicated the front door with his head.

Sergeant Greene tucked his cell phone away.

"Here's how we're going to play this," Asher stated. "Maddy, Justin, and I will walk you all out. They'll snap a few photos, shout a few questions. Sergeant, you tell them it was a malfunctioning gate and security breach, and that has now become a trespassing issue. I'll press charges against anyone who is not off my property within five minutes. Is that clear? We'll all be very friendly." He gave them his most charming smile.

Justin tilted his head. "Ah, we're blaming this on them? Brilliant, boss."

The sergeant gave them a harassed glance. "I'll need to call the lieutenant back; he's on his way."

Asher frowned at the man shuffling his feet, refusing to make eye contact.

"This lieutenant of yours, he wouldn't speak to the press, would he?" Asher said, "He's not going to make this more difficult to explain, just to see himself on television?"

A quick glance at the expressions ranging from pained to amused on the other officers' faces told him all he needed to know.

"We're not waiting for him."

Sergeant Greene made a token sound of protest.

Asher held up a hand. "Does everyone know their roles?" he barked.

There were nods all around.

He turned to Maddy. "You. Love struck. Hero worship."

She laughed, then sobered and said quietly, "Your mom?"

He stiffened. "I'll deal with her."

"She has a gun, Asher," she whispered so quietly in his ear he could barely hear her.

Fuck. That bitch. So, she showed Maddy her Derringer?

He pulled Maddy away and gave her a gentle shake. "Trust me. I'll take care of it."

She relaxed imperceptibly.

"Justin?"

He grinned. "Ready, boss."

He surveyed the glum group surrounding him.

"Smiles, everyone. Smiles!" He gave them his thousand-megawatt grin and they filed zthrough the front door, led by Justin.

Asher pulled Maddy up against his body as they made their way awkwardly down the steps together. There must have been twenty-five people there with cameras. Some with badges. Most of them appeared to have slept in their clothes. Asher shook his head, grin firmly in place. *Parasites.*

Sergeant Greene shouted, "Listen up, people. The security gate malfunctioned. The homeowner called us. I've got reinforcements on the way and will be citing for trespass. Just because the gate was open doesn't mean you're allowed to enter. This is private property. Now get out." The three other officers started ushering the photographers down the driveway.

Someone shouted, "We heard it was a domestic dispute!"

"Yeah!" someone else echoed.

That was his cue. He pulled Maddy's resistant body into his arms and kissed her. Really kissed her with his lips, tongue, and breath. She clutched at his shoulders and he was totally lost.

The sound of Justin's laughter recalled him moments later. He lifted his head, dazed. Far from leaving, the paparazzi were catcalling and, most of all, snapping photo after photo of him and Maddy. He glanced down and grinned, a real honest-to-God happy grin.

Her gaze was unfocused, with no trace of self-consciousness despite the audience of their press.

He grabbed Sergeant Greene's arm.

"I'll let you take it from here. I have things to attend to."
Sergeant Greene laughed.

• • •

An hour later he left a sleeping Maddy in his bed and made the call to his father.

"Sterling Lowe."

"It's Asher."

"Is Ella okay?"

"Ella's fine. I'm calling because that batshit-crazy bitch kidnapped Maddy at gunpoint."

"What?"

"Yeah. Apparently she's still got that Derringer."

"That shouldn't have happened. I've got people on her."

"You do?"

"Of course. How do you think I managed to keep her away from you all these years?"

"Well, I'm heading over there to—"

"Don't. I'm not going to tell you your business, but it'd be best if you let me handle this."

"No."

Sterling sighed. "Please, Asher. She *wants* your attention. She's like a child. If you give it to her, you let her know that is how she can get to you, and she'll continue to try to get you through the people you love. That could mean Ella, too. Any interaction fuels her. I have this on the best authority. But I can make sure it doesn't happen again. You have my word."

"I need to be *sure* she won't try anything, with Maddy or Ella."

"It's as important to me as it is to you. She's not healthy, Asher. She never has been."

"Would she try anything with Ella?"

"Taking her?"

"Yeah."

"It's possible. With her anything is possible." His tone underwent a subtle change. "You're too close to Jacqueline in L.A., Asher. Ella would be safer here with me."

Here come the machinations.

"Forget it, Sterling. If you can't take care of Jacqueline, the police—"

"No. I'll tighten up security on her and keep her occupied with something else. I can usually create enough drama to suck her attention away somehow."

He was surprised the man was admitting to being so manipulative.

"If she creates another problem for me, I'll go public with her mental illness, press charges about kidnapping Maddy, all of it."

Sterling sighed. "That won't do any good, but I'll keep better tabs. You have my word."

Asher padded back to the bedroom where Maddy was awake and stretching.

"We need to talk," she said, solemnly, fluffing the pillow behind her and leaning back.

She watched him approach, top button of his jeans unbuttoned, shirtless. "I know. I'm sorry, Maddy. I had no idea—she's never done anything like this before. It has been a dozen years since I've had contact with her. I just talked to Sterling about it. He's been keeping tabs on her; he thinks maybe the press about Ella or you in my life set her off. Or maybe she came off her medications? But it's being taken care of. "

She sat up and folded her arms around her sheet-covered knees. "Yeah. Well, good. I'd hate for Ella to be in her sights. But,

I'm more concerned about you. Your willingness to accept that I would break up with you because people said nasty things about me. And on the phone? I would never."

"Maddy, I haven't dated many women unaccustomed to celebrity. Nearly all of my relationships have been with women who knew what they were getting into with me—in fact, for many of them, dating in the public eye was more of a perk than a hindrance. I've kept a pretty low profile since Dee died. Deliberately. And I should've warned you that there would be nastiness once you were publicly linked with me. I'm sorry."

She tensed and hugged her knees to her chest. "Because I'm not up to your usual standard?"

He made a choked sound and she looked up, affronted.

"Maddy, you are so far and away above my usual standard, it's laughable."

It was as though the wind had been knocked out of her; a warmth settled in her chest. It wasn't a declaration of love but it was some kind of declaration, and she reveled in it.

"After Dee's death I lost interest in doing a lot of the things I normally enjoyed—the parties...uh...the women."

She reached for his hand and he gripped it tightly. "You were struggling."

"You met me at my lowest point. I've been in a successful band for two decades. I've experienced burnout—from the road, groupies, conflicts within the band—you name it." He played with the fingers on her hand. She winced and he dropped it, and gathered her into his lap with a sympathetic sound. "I'm not complaining. But when Dee died...I've never experienced anything like that. For a while I was numb. But things are better now. So much better with the two of you."

She wrapped an arm around him and traced the raised, inflamed skin over his shoulder blade, a newly inked Celtic symbol with something that looked vaguely like the number four upside-down, entwined within. "Were you going to mention this?"

His shoulder twitched under her ministrations.

She moved her hand to the nape of his neck and stroked him. "Dee?"

"Yeah."

He leaned back until she was straddling him; he laced his fingers through her hair and pulled her down to his mouth.

Chapter 17

Asher put the guitar down and checked his messages. He'd missed a flurry of calls from his attorney and held the phone to his ear to listen to the message the man had left. Minutes later his guitar lay in pieces around him in his home studio. If there was ever a rock musician voted least likely to smash up a perfectly good Gibson, it was Asher Lowe. Cars? Hotel rooms? Most certainly. Guitars? Never.

At this rate he'd be headed to anger management classes. Not that it would be necessary, as it appeared he was on the verge of losing custody of Ella. With a dim sense of unreality, he entered his office and picked up the documents his attorney had faxed and skimmed them.

"Fuck."

He took the sheaf of papers to the living room to await Maddy's return from the store. He looked through the papers again, numb with disbelief. His attorney called back; there would be an emergency hearing, but it hadn't been scheduled.

By the time he heard the slam of the front door, it felt as though he'd been waiting hours for Maddy to return.

"Asher." She halted mid-step, staring at him. "What's happened?" she whispered. "Is it Ella?"

He stood, holding up the sheaf of papers in a hand that trembled.

"Is this how he did it?"

Maddy was close enough to see her mother's bank logo on the front of the top piece of paper. He watched her closely. Despite the mounting evidence, he'd held on to a frisson of hope. But there it was, a damning flash of guilt across her face before she looked away.

Something tore inside, a physical pain accompanied the
evisceration of his heart. He'd actually fallen in love with her, he
realized with dawning horror. He'd always been so careful not to get
too deeply involved. Not to lose himself in a woman, not to trust
like that. And now that he had, she would cost him everything.
Disbelief and pain were morphing back into fury. God knew what
showed on his face, but inside, searing rage raced through him.

She held up a hand, beseechingly.

"How could you do this to me? To Ella?" he gritted.

"Asher, your dad contacted me but—"

"Oh I know," he replied, in a voice so bitter he barely recognized
it as his own, "an emergency custody hearing has been scheduled.
My attorney tells me you've been busy keeping my father up to
date with all my failings. Sterling knows all of it, and he'll leverage
it to take custody from me. You…you…deceitful bitch," he heard
her gasp, but continued, raggedly, "you know how hard I tried—"
his voice broke and he turned away.

He was really losing it, on the cusp of throwing shit around
again.

He heard her behind him, too close.

"Asher, that's not what—I didn't. That is, he asked, but…if you
would just listen—"

He whirled, "We'll all get to listen to you, in court. Get out of
my house."

She shrank from the expression on his face. With a small sound,
she turned on her heel and fled the room. He heard the front door
shut moments later.

God help him. She knew everything. He had told her things
he had never shared with another soul, his feelings of betrayal
and anger mixed with regret about his relationship with Dee.
She *knew* him. She knew his *history*. Why did she do it? Money?

She wouldn't put Ella's welfare aside because of blackmail. Not her.

He tamped down the voice that told him he should have helped her mother. His investigation had turned up her mother's straitened circumstances. But he hadn't wanted the awkwardness that accompanied such a gift to cause a rift or some perceived imbalance in their status. He'd gifted people with money over the years, and it always put a strain on the relationship. The last thing he wanted from Maddy was gratitude; she had enough concerns about the disparity of their incomes and her employment.

Maddy had joined forces with Sterling against him. All but handed Ella to his father. And there could only be one reason she would do that. She thought Sterling would make a better guardian. That twisted him up in agonizing knots of self-doubt and pain. She'd had valid concerns about his parenting and interest in Ella the first few weeks—he'd fucked up royally before coming out of his funk—but Ella had come to mean the world to him. How could Maddy not know that? And why would she do it this way?

He stalked over to the bar and poured himself a giant tumbler of Scotch and drank most of it in one long swallow—desperate to numb the pain. Putting the glass down, he pitched himself onto the sofa and covered his face with shaking hands. What was he thinking? Ella would be home in a few hours, and he couldn't show up drunk at the bus stop.

He gritted his teeth and pulled out his cell phone. Eyes stinging, he concentrated on slowing his breathing.

His father answered with "Is Ella all right?"

"I wanted you to know I fired your little spy."

There was a sharp sound from the other end.

"You bastard," Asher said.

"Asher, listen to me—"

"*No.* You listen. How dare you? You and your games. You used her mom's *house* to blackmail her? Her mother's livelihood? And you think you'll make a better role model than *me*, you sick fuck?" he spat out.

It was as though someone hit him in the stomach with a two by four. He could have sworn his feelings for Maddy were the real thing. He would have bet she reciprocated them. He'd let her in, and she knew how hard he was trying. And it still wasn't good enough. He couldn't even begin to think about losing Ella.

"I'm not sorry," Sterling said. "I'll go to any lengths to make sure Ella is okay. And son, you *have* to know she'd be better off with me. If there's anything you've learned the last few months, it's that you can't care for a child. I know, Asher. All of it. Losing her at the store? Keeping her up late?"

She told his father everything.

"It's too much for you. Give her to me."

Asher's body went still. The hair rose on the back of his neck.

"You're still the same. I made choices you didn't agree with, so I'm useless? I didn't follow in your footsteps, so I must be a fuck up? You're the only person on the planet who sees me as a fuck up. Ella's far better off with me, and Dee knew it. That's why she didn't change her will. I'll never let you get custody. You're a bully and a lousy dad, and given half a chance you'll wreck this little girl the way you tried to wreck me and Dee. You have no idea how to be a father. *None.* Take it from me."

"That's the thing, son. I don't want what happened to you to happen to Ella. I don't want her to be…damaged."

Asher gave a short, humorless laugh. "*I'm* damaged?"

"You are a lousy guardian for Ella for the same reasons I was a lousy parent. You can't put her ahead of yourself. You neglect her for business, a phone call."

"Oh, the irony."

"Yes. The irony. I will take her from you at the hearing. I've rearranged my life to care for that little girl."

Asher scowled. "As have I."

His father continued as if he hadn't heard. "I'll give her my all, Asher. I should have done it with you and Dee. I didn't know. I can't let you make the same mistakes I made."

"I'll see you in court." Asher disconnected the phone.

He picked up the nearest object, ready to hurl it into the wall, but stopped. He looked at the thing in his hand. A travel mug Maddy made for him with photos of Delilah and Ella. He put it down and collapsed onto the couch, staring at it.

The anger faded, leaving heartache in its wake.

Chapter 18

When Maddy's cell phone rang at eight A.M. her heart leaped. Asher? Maybe he would let her explain. She should have told him about Sterling's initial call, but since she'd decided early on not to help him, she hadn't seen the need to. Besides, she'd discussed the matter of the phone call with Ella's therapist. The woman had been adamant that Maddy stay out of it—completely out of it. She had instructed Maddy to keep silent about Sterling's phone call and offer. The therapist didn't want to add fuel to Asher's anger toward his father. The woman held out hope for reconciliation between Sterling and Asher, if only for Ella's sake.

But how could Sterling possibly have the information he did? Had someone been following them?

She focused on the number and her shoulders slumped. Not Asher.

"Hello?"

"Madeline Anderson?"

"Yes?"

"This is Patricia Leeds from the Los Angeles County Family Services court. We need you to testify today at an emergency hearing to discuss the welfare of Ella Lowe."

"That's *today*?"

"Are you the child's nanny?"

"Yes. I mean, I was."

"What dates were you employed?"

Maddy gave the woman the information.

"So you quit yesterday?"

"Quit? Not exactly," Maddy hedged.

There was a weary sigh from the other end of the phone. "Do you know where the courthouse is?"

"Yes."

"Then we'll see you at eleven A.M. this morning. Third floor, conference room eleven."

"Okay." Maddy put the phone down on the coffee table and sat staring into space.

She hadn't the energy yesterday to put her things away, and today she was so exhausted and heartsick she was almost catatonic. Getting up, she checked the kitchen cabinets for coffee. Ah, good, there was half a bag of beans.

She hadn't done her usual stretches this morning, so she had zero flexibility and a lot of pain. She ground the beans and put them in the bottom of the French press then put the kettle on and waited until the whistle sounded.

Her chest ached; her swollen eyes burned as tears of grief and shame welled in them. The kettle whistled at full throttle. Maddy absently turned the burner knob to off and poured the boiling water. Too fast. It sloshed over the back of her hand holding the handle of the press.

"Ouch. Damn it." She pulled her hand away and set down the kettle. She stared at the burned flesh. If it was red and painful, it would blister. That's all she needed. Scars on her ugly hands. Good. Maybe the soreness from the burn and the pain in her body could distract her from the ache in her heart.

• • •

Maddy pushed the button in the courthouse elevator at ten forty-five. The doors opened, depositing her on the third floor. She walked stiffly down the linoleum hallway, checking doors for numbers. Wrong corridor. She turned back with a sigh, clutching her purse with sweaty hands. A white bandage on her left hand covered the angry half dollar–size blister. Conference room eleven. She walked in warily.

There was Sterling Lowe, impeccably attired in a gray suit, sitting next to a man that must be his lawyer. Asher was at the opposite end of the table, his back to her. She could see his spine stiffen as she walked in, but he didn't turn. Her heart clenched. The only other occupants were the therapist and the social worker, talking quietly together on the far side of the room. They each turned a sympathetic smile in her direction.

Maddy made her way to a chair in the middle of the oval conference table, pulled it out and sat down. Purse in her lap, she stared at her hands, unwilling to meet Asher's eyes. Dread formed a cold, hard knot where her stomach used to be.

The black-robed female judge came in the room, followed by a harried-looking fiftyish woman juggling files and a computer. Belatedly Maddy rose to her feet after the others while the judge and her assistant settled themselves. She could feel Asher's eyes on her and peeked through the curtain of her hair. His eyes were coldly furious, promising retribution.

Maddy swallowed hard and studied the table. The social worker she had only met once and the therapist settled into chairs next to each other on Maddy's right side.

The judge's lips twisted. "I see here we're due in court in less than a month. Anyone care to tell me why we're here early?" She gave a hard look to the social worker, and then turned her gaze on the therapist.

Sterling Lowe's attorney cleared his throat. "Judge, if I may?"

She glared him down. "No, you may not. I'd like to hear from the women in the room, since they, at least, are *supposed* to be impartial and only concerned about the welfare of the child."

Asher made a sound that could've been a snort. The judge whipped her head around. The court reporter continued to type, head down.

Mimi, the social worker, piped up. "Mr. Lowe…er…Mr. Sterling Lowe, brought some incidents to our attention."

"Let's hear it," the judge barked. "I don't have all day."

"According to Mr. Lowe Senior, Mr. Asher Lowe lost the child in a mall."

The judge looked over her glasses at Asher. "True?"

Asher gave a curt nod, glowering.

"For how long?" the judge asked.

"Fifteen minutes."

The judge shook her head. "It happens. Probably the longest fifteen minutes of your life, am I right?"

Asher sat back, clearly off guard. "As a matter of fact, yeah. Your Honor."

Sterling Lowe leaned forward, flushed with rage. "Not to my grandchild, it doesn't!" he thundered. The attorney tugged on his arm.

Sterling shook him off.

The judge narrowed her eyes at Asher's father. "You're doing yourself no favors." She pointed at the attorney next to Sterling. "Tell him."

Sterling's high-priced attorney dragged a finger under his collar and whispered to his client.

The judge surveyed Asher, then Sterling. "It happens to the best of us." Directing her gaze at Asher she said, "I assume you did all the right things to find her?"

He nodded.

"Including panicking, screaming her name, and running around like a chicken with your head cut off?"

Asher's eyes widened. "Yep." His attorney nudged him. "Your Honor."

The judge turned a dour expression on Sterling. "Save putting children on leashes—something I'm not opposed to in some instances—that's gonna happen. What else?"

Mimi responded haltingly, "Well, apparently the child urinated in public."

Wait. *What?* Maddy sat forward in her chair. How could he possibly have known that about Ella peeing on the street? Had they been followed? This wasn't making any sense. Nausea twisted through Maddy.

Sterling Lowe sat back, a smug expression on his face.

"That was my fault," Maddy blurted.

"And you are?" She turned her narrow gaze to Maddy.

"I'm the…I was…Ella's nanny."

"Hmmmph. So what happened?"

"We had a play date and the woman wouldn't let us in. Ella had to go…" Maddy shrugged. "But it wasn't a busy street, just a residential one, and there was no other option."

The judge looked over her glasses at Sterling and shook her head. "Whole lotta nothin' here."

"There are a number of other incidents," Sterling's lawyer interjected, flipping through the sheaf of papers in front of him.

"I thought I told you to stay out of it." She glared at the attorney. "I have the motion in front of me."

"Yes, ma'am."

She next directed her steely gaze at Maddy. "Do I need to place the child elsewhere?"

"Oh no!" Maddy gasped. "Please don't. Ella," she glanced at Asher, "Ella loves her uncle. She may love her grandfather, too, but she's doing so well with us. Uh…with him."

Sterling Lowe interrupted. "Of course she'd say that. She's sleeping with him."

Funny how you could still hear people's reactions when they didn't make a sound.

Asher's jaw was clenched, face expressionless.

The judge made a derisive sound.

Maddy felt the anger steadily creeping up, threatening to overwhelm her. "Yes. I'm…I was sleeping with him. I care for Asher, but that's not the point of this hearing, is it? We're supposed to be doing what's best for Ella. And you," she pointed a shaking finger at Sterling Lowe, "I don't know how you got your information. The *only* people who knew about those incidents were me and Asher and—" her mouth dropped open, "—my mom. I sent her e-mails about what's going on," she said. "Good God. You've hacked my e-mail!"

Sterling Lowe didn't have the grace to look ashamed. His attorney cleared his throat but remained silent.

Maddy looked daggers at them and then turned to the judge. "I shared some of our struggles with my mom. We're close and she runs a daycare. I ask her advice from time to time," she explained. "Maybe I shouldn't have, but my mom is great with kids. She even has some experience with children and grief. I never meant…how could he?" She looked back to the judge. "He has my e-mails. Is that legal?"

In her peripheral vision she saw Asher sitting forward in his chair; she could feel the eyes of everyone in the room on her.

The judge was contemplating Asher's father. His attorney was looking around the room. With a sigh, the judge turned back to Maddy.

"Of course it's not legal. Not that I can waste county money going after him for it." She jerked her head in Sterling's direction. "It would be difficult to prove and only result in a fine anyway. But it shows very poor judgment."

She turned her attention to the therapist. "How is the child adjusting?"

The woman shot a nervous look at Sterling.

Was he blackmailing her, too?

The woman held up both her hands. "Ella's doing beautifully, all things considered. She loves school, she loves Maddy, and she's coming to love her uncle. She misses her grandfather and she still struggles with the loss of her mom. In a perfect world, I'd like to see both these men who love Ella care for her. But I can see why that's impossible. I don't know who would be the best guardian for Ella, but I strongly advise against another upheaval or major change at this time. It's my recommendation that guardianship remain with Asher Lowe."

The social worker nodded her assent. "As long as we're recommending what's best for the child, I don't think it's another nanny. Regardless of their…er…personal issues, Ella has bonded with Maddy, and it's a very strong bond. One I don't advise breaking, given everything the child has been through."

Maddy stared at the table fighting tears, thankful her hair was a curtain around her face.

The judge pursed her lips and slapped her hands flat on the table.

"I've heard enough. The child stays with Asher Lowe. Mr. Lowe, I don't care what your personal situation is with Ms. Anderson. It's lamentable that you couldn't keep your hands off your employee, but maybe now we can carry on a professional relationship?"

Maddy instinctively nodded.

Asher did not respond.

"But we're going to do what's best for the child here, and that is Ms. Anderson. Is that clear?"

"Yes, ma'am," Asher drawled.

"Ms. Anderson?"

Maddy swallowed hard. She peeked over at Asher.

He was staring at her, expressionless.

"Yes, Your Honor. I'd like to continue to care for Ella."

The judge turned to Sterling Lowe. "Mr. Lowe. Clearly you are a man used to getting what you want by subverting the rules." She raised a dismissive hand. "That may work in your world, but it doesn't work in mine. Where children and families are concerned, we care about the character of those providing for them. You're no spring chicken, so I'm certain my words are falling on deaf ears, but if you pulled this 'end justifies the means' nonsense with your children, it's no wonder you're estranged."

"I love Ella. I want what's best for her," Sterling Lowe said, hoarsely.

The room was silent, every pair of eyes on the older man at the end of the table.

The judge continued in a softer tone. "Yes. All of us here understand that. In fact, believe it or not, every single one of us in this room wants that. And everyone *but* you believes that Ella is getting the love and care she needs in her current environment. So when you are the sole outlier, you need to consider that your desires may be in conflict with reality. You'd be best off mending fences with your son."

Asher made a sound—a derisive snort?—and covered quickly with a cough.

• • •

Maddy walked out of the conference room, brushing at the tears continuously leaking from her eyes.

"Maddy." She recognized Asher's authoritative tone and picked up her pace. She'd call him later, after she got herself under control.

She turned the corner and spotted the door to a handicapped bathroom. She dashed in but the door was slow to close, so she tugged the handle. A large male hand wrapped around the upper part of the door, pulling it out of her grasp. Asher pushed her inside the dark, tiled room and locked the door. Her vision was slow to adjust to the dim light, but she eyed him warily.

He raked a hand through his hair.

"What do you want?" she said.

"To apologize."

He stepped toward her, and she backed up into the wall.

She looked around. Drat. She could just make out the light switch on the other side of him.

"Maddy. I'm sorry I assumed the worst, but you have to admit—"

"I don't admit anything. I told you I didn't betray you. You wanted to believe the worst of me. You didn't even give me a chance to explain."

"I know."

"I don't want to discuss it with you. I'll come back to care for Ella, but that's all."

He took another half step forward.

Her back was to the cold wall so she put a hand up to ward him off.

"Damn it, Maddy. I'm sorry. More sorry than you could ever imagine."

Her eyes were adjusting to the dark room, illuminated only by the sliver of light coming under the door. He was close enough that she could see the remorse in his expression. "Will you please just give me a chance to apologize?"

Her stomach clenched. "Fine," she said, curtly. "You did. Now get out."

"Maddy." She examined him more closely. He looked terrible. Strung out. Worse than he had been the first weeks he had Ella. "I'm sorry I misjudged you," he spread his hands, "I just figured you thought Sterling would do a better job than me."

"*What?*"

"Well, once I calmed down, I realized you weren't the type of person who gives in to blackmail. The only thing that made sense was that I'd made so many mistakes you didn't think I was able to…" his voice broke and he rubbed his eyes, "cut it as her guardian. And that you couldn't tell me because of our…because of our relationship."

She pulled his hand down.

His expression was stark.

"How could you even think that?" She grabbed his upper arms and gave him a little shake. "You're doing great. I'll admit I had real qualms at first, but you've stepped up. And, even if I did still have concerns, I'd *tell* you, not go behind your back!"

"I know. I *know*. But the information he had. There was no way it could have come from anyone *but* you—fucking Sterling, I should've known. Can you forgive me?"

In answer she wrapped her arms around his neck and urged his mouth to hers. The kiss started out softly, tentatively apologetic. One large hand came up to cup her jaw. His lips stroked hers again, then again while his other hand ran down her back in a long caress.

With an impatient sound, she fisted her hand in his silky hair and held his head. She was starving for him.

His mouth muffled her moans, his hips pressed her into the wall and she struggled to get closer as she rubbed herself against his pants. She could feel his huge erection straining against her as his free hand went under her tailored shirt, under her soft, cotton camisole to hold her breast. She whimpered against his lips, gripping the back of his head, her tongue searching for and finding his. His long, skilled fingers played with first one nipple, then the other. His free hand went to her hips to grind her harder against the hot strength of his arousal. Grabbing his hand, she dragged it down, over her stomach, lower, to the hem of her skirt. She maneuvered it, up the inside of her trembling thigh. She let go and he continued the journey, yanking her panties down and cupping her with his broad palm.

Maddy whimpered, her hands clawing at his back.

He locked his mouth to hers as he stroked her clit. Rubbing the sensitive nub in small circles with his thumb, his two long fingers pumped into her. The orgasm came, hard and fast. She threw her head back, banging it against the wall as she came with a cry that turned into a yelp, echoing off the tile in the bathroom.

He held her slack form against the wall with his body. His fingers still inside her intermittently pulsing body, he palmed the back of her head with his other hand, pulled her forehead to his, never breaking eye contact, and sang softly in his unmistakable baritone, "I'll give you all, if you let me."

She shivered, a full body ripple. "Not here you won't, not in a damn restroom." Her eyes narrowed. "Is that a Spade lyric I should know?"

He released her and smoothed her clothing. "Something I'm working on." He cast a look behind him. "Looks pretty clean to me."

"Your standards must be very low. I'm certain you've done it in worse places," she grumbled.

He laughed. "If I have, I never enjoyed it so much."

Maddy laid her head on the soft cotton of his dress shirt and listened to his heart gallop.

His body was immobile, but she could still feel him pressed against her. She raised her head.

His flushed face was deadly serious. "God, Maddy. I'm really sorry."

"We told the judge we wouldn't do this."

He released her, reluctantly.

"Yeah, well, *I* didn't. Nothing has changed. I don't think it's a bad thing for Ella to see us together."

"Until we aren't."

"Maddy, this is not casual. I'm crazy about you. Even when I thought you'd betrayed me, I couldn't get you out of my head. Apparently my feelings for you don't have an off switch."

That had to be the least romantic declaration ever made, but her heart leapt at his words.

She gave him a withering look. "Just so we're clear. If I have a problem, Ella related or not, I'll tell you. I don't care if you're my lover, my employer, my favorite singer or all three, you will know where you stand with me."

A little twinge of guilt twisted in her and made forgiveness a whole lot easier. She had considered it, before she knew him.

• • •

An hour later she called her mom from Asher's house.

"Maddy love!" Her mother's overjoyed voice came over the line. "I was going to call you a little later. You sitting down? I got some good news this afternoon. I'm not sure of the specifics, but apparently some veteran's supporter paid off the house. It's one of the private programs to help wives of men killed in service to their country. They had a benefactor and I was one of the people selected. Can you believe it? The bank called this morning."

"Wow," Maddy said. "I mean, congratulations."

Asher.

Mrs. Anderson laughed. "Maddy, it's like a miracle. I was really in trouble."

"What?"

"Oh, I guess it doesn't matter if you know. I couldn't refinance when my rates went up a few years ago, and I was only making partial payments. They didn't allow me to restructure the loan. I was in deep trouble, Maddy."

"Oh, Mom. You should've told me."

"What could you have done?"

What indeed.

"I'm overjoyed. I'm going to meet the Stuarts tonight to celebrate."

Maddy attempted a few more happy sounds. Her mother was too excited to notice.

Maddy walked into the kitchen and sat across from Asher at the kitchen table. She put the phone down and sized him up. "I guess a thank you is in order? I'm not sure how I feel about it."

Asher cocked his head over his burrito.

"I'm not following, babe."

"My mom. Her mortgage."

"I was going to talk to you about that this morning. You know I'm happy to pay it off, Maddy. Just wondering how best to do it. Your mom has an excess of pride. Could I give you the money to give to her?"

Was this an act? She studied him, chewing his food. "She called this morning. It's been paid."

He dropped the burrito onto the plate. "Motherfucker," he said, through a mouthful of carne asada.

Maddy's eyes widened as the other possibility dawned. "Sterling?"

"Who else?" he asked bitterly.

Chapter 19

Maddy stretched on her lounge chair on the sunny patio. It was a cloudless day, warm in the sun, cool in the shade—typical L.A. winter weather. She hugged herself, trying to remember when she'd been so happy. Despite her reservations about getting involved in a relationship with Asher, everything fit together. Ella was thriving.

The questions about Dee continued of course, and she still grieved, but the nightmares were few and far between. It was achingly sad and reassuring that Ella was moving past the desperate grief of losing her mother. Asher still couldn't bring himself to go through Dee's things, but he had asked Maddy to do it. She'd planned to go through the boxes today and made a mental note to ask the therapist if she could share some of the items with Ella.

Now that she knew Asher better, she understood the magnitude of his loss. Dee was one of only a handful of people in his life he was close to, and their sibling bond had been forged through their parents' respective marriages and divorces, through nannies and prep schools and rebellions against their father. In many ways, taking care of his sister in his youth had paved the way for taking care of her child.

Maddy made her way up to one of the many guest rooms. Each had a seasonal theme and the boxes were stored in the "fall" guest room, her personal favorite. The walls were a beautiful sage green, the black-and-white prints on the wall were exquisite, the linens in shades of chocolate brown with orange accents. She pulled the top off the first box—a Bankers Box—stuffed full of papers. There were mostly bills, neatly organized by month, going back a few years. No mementos, nothing personal. She put the top back and put it aside. The second box was more of a trunk. It contained beautiful scarves; a faux fur wrap; a barely used, giant designer handbag; and a diaper bag.

Maddy pulled this last item out and stared at it. She opened it and dug her fingers into its cavernous interior. A cold metal object with a plastic tip met her fingertips and she fished it out. A baby spoon.

There was something in one of the pockets too substantial to be a diaper. Frowning, she pulled it out of the pocket. It was a little red book, thin and slightly larger than a paperback novel, with no writing on the outside. Each page was filled with blue inked words. Maddy sat back on her heels. A journal? She held it shut between her palms. Huh. She flipped through the pages again, peering at the tiny script. She opened it to the first page. No name, no information about the owner, just the brand printed on the bottom left inside cover.

Maybe Asher should read it. But what if there was personal information in there that Dee didn't want her family to know? Shouldn't Maddy at least ask someone? She read the first page. Nothing too risqué—not on the first page at any rate—and it was very stream of consciousness. She set it aside and quickly went through the other boxes looking for journals. Among the mementos, photos, and memorabilia she found three more books tucked away. She restacked the boxes and sat with the four red books in front of her.

Then she called him. "Asher?"

"Hey, babe."

"Sweetie, listen, I was going through Delilah's stuff…"

"Yeah?"

"I found some journals."

There was silence on the other end of the phone.

"What do you want me to do?" she asked.

"Have you read them?" His tone was sharp.

"Of course not. I found them and called you."

When he spoke again his voice was unutterably weary. "I guess we can't burn them, can we?"

"Asher, it's one of the few links Ella has to her mother."

"I know. But what if there's negative stuff in there?"

"About?"

"Me. My dad. Her old lifestyle. She was a party girl until she got pregnant with Ella. Stuff a brother doesn't want to know about his sister."

"Only one way to find out."

"Can you read them, please? If she writes about things she wouldn't want Ella to see, get rid of it, will you? Like if she talks about being upset that she's pregnant or—"

"I understand."

"I hate to put this on you."

"Don't worry. It's not hard for me. I didn't know and love her the way you all did."

Asher sighed. "I know it's a lot to ask, but if there's—well, if she writes stuff I don't need to know, don't tell me, okay?"

"Okay, babe."

"Even if I insist."

"I know," she said softly.

It took a few tries but she finally got the journals in chronological order. The first one Dee had kept intermittently for several months for an English project in high school, then two she kept through college. Ill-fated relationships, her troubled relationship with her father, her distant relationship with her mother, classes, trips, Asher. It was all there.

Unlike the others, the last journal had huge gaps of time. It was started a few years after college when she was very social, and it ended before Ella's birth. Maddy got a real sense of who Dee was, and knew she would've liked her. She was almost through the last book when she read a sentence. She read it again. All the air rushed out of her lungs and she put a hand to her forehead, lightheaded.

She closed the journal and put it away from her on the floor. No, she had read that wrong. Maddy picked it up and flipped through to find the line again. This time she continued to read the journal through to the end and then flipped back to that fateful page, staring at it with a dawning sense of horror.

There it was in black and white. Ella's father's name. Printed in Delilah's loopy script. Maddy considered putting all the journals away, hiding them. Burning them. This one at least.

Oh God.

Dee hadn't revealed much about him in the journal, just his name and that he was a contractor in Las Vegas. A fling with a man totally removed from her world and her friends; a chance meeting at a bar that led to a long, sex-filled weekend in a motel.

Why hadn't she told him? Maybe she was afraid he would reject her and the baby or turn something casual into something serious because of the Lowe money. Whatever the reason, she didn't write it down. She didn't mention him throughout the rest of the journal. The last few pages were filled with the excitement of a newly pregnant woman and plans for the future.

What on earth should she do with this information? Asher had to be told. Her hand holding the journal tightened until it was painful. Sometimes doing the right thing could be disastrous.

She picked up her phone and dialed. "Asher?"

"Hey, babe. What's up?"

"Can you come home?"

"What, Maddy? I'm in the middle of a few things here."

"It's urgent and I don't want to talk about it on the phone."

"On my way; be there in twenty."

She was sitting on the sectional in the living room when he arrived, a glass of water untouched on the coffee table in front of her, the red journal in her hand.

He eyed it warily. "Is that it?"

"This is one of four, the most recent one. It ends just before she delivered Ella."

He stood in front of her, staring at the journal as though it were a poisonous toad.

"There's nothing bad in here—in any of them—about you, Asher. She obviously loved you, counted on you, and trusted you. She was conflicted about a lot of things—her relationship with her parents, boyfriends, her career or lack thereof, her friends—but she's very clear about how much she loved you."

He covered his mouth with a shaking hand. "I wish I'd been around more, especially the last few years." He dragged his hands through his hair. "I thought I'd have more time."

Maddy blinked away tears, and Asher sat next to her on the edge of the couch.

He turned to face her. "What is it?"

"Ella's dad," she said, softly.

He reared back.

"She names Ella's dad."

"No fucking way." He nearly ripped the journal from her hands.

She helped him find the page.

His searching eyes found the passage immediately. He read. And kept reading. The hands holding the book started to shake.

Maddy leaned into him, trying to provide the comfort of her body.

He held her to him absently, and fell back into the couch as he continued to read.

When he finished, he went back to the passage where she mentioned Ella's dad by name. He sat for a few minutes, silently staring at the page, no doubt cursing the name. Finally, with a sigh he pulled his cell phone out of his pocket, hit a contact and was connected to his attorney, then his attorney's investigator. Asher gave the man on the other end of the phone brief instructions. Check him out. Check out the family. Immediately and thoroughly. Report back as soon as possible. Asher hung up and held Maddy close.

"She must've had a good reason for keeping Ella from him," Maddy whispered. "Right?"

"I would think so. But if she did, she doesn't mention it."

"What are we going to do?"

They exchanged worried glances. "We'll see what turns up. I'm not letting Ella go," he stated.

Maddy's stomach tightened into a knot. "Do you think your dad—"

"No. We both pressed her to tell us who he was. She wouldn't have told my dad and not me."

"What did she say when you asked?"

"She told me it could have been one of several guys." He cleared his throat. "It was pretty awkward. I know a lot about my sister, and far be it from me to cast stones, given my history with women, but there are things I don't want to know."

Maddy indicated the journal. "It seems she was pretty serious with someone in college."

"Yeah. Phillip Mitchell. He was a good guy, but overwhelmed by the Lowe name. She was in love with love. Nothing lasting after Phil, at least not that I knew of. She went through a real partying stage right up until she got pregnant. Some of the people she hung out with?" He shuddered. "I don't know this guy, Ben Logan, but if he's anything like the rest of them, he's a flake."

"Maybe he is. Maybe he isn't. He wasn't part of her crowd. And if he was a flake, it's been six years. He could've changed. Your sister matured after becoming responsible for a child."

He leaned back and frowned. "Whose side are you on?"

"Ella's," she said, firmly, "and doing the right thing."

"No one is taking her from us."

"I'll admit, I'm hoping he's got a criminal record a mile long or worse."

That coaxed a smile from him. "What's worse?"

"Are you going to contact your dad?" She hated even bringing him up, given their history with his father.

"Not yet." He squeezed her. "I'm going to check out this Ben guy first."

Chapter 20

Maddy hoped never to live through another week like this last one. The phone rang constantly, and with each report Asher grew more distant. He was too strung out for any kind of intimacy—coming home late, getting up late. He spent all his time in the studio. Classic avoidance, shades of her first weeks. She'd given him space; he seemed to need it to process what he had to do. Tonight Asher had finally gotten home in time to see Ella. She heard the front door slam closed as she was starting the bedtime routine.

"Ella, I'm going to send your uncle up."

She made her way down the stairs and found him in the kitchen.

Maddy put a hand on his arm. "Asher, will you put Ella to bed? She's been asking for you."

He glanced over his shoulder toward the kitchen then gave her what passed for a smile these days.

"Yeah. Of course. I just need to—" He looked over his shoulder again.

"Uncle Asher?" Ella called from the top of the stairs.

He took the stairs two at a time and swung her up in his arms. Maddy heard the squeals and smiled to herself as she walked into the kitchen.

On the kitchen island sat a thick manila file and three of the four journals. He had been tightlipped and impatient with her queries about the investigation into Ben. One-word responses or grunts.

I shouldn't.

Screw it. She opened the file and stood reading. She read the reports all the way through, then restarted, skimming. Financials, photos, and notes on Ben, and from what she could tell, nearly everyone in the family. Interviews with neighbors. It was incredibly thorough.

She gathered the items and went to sit in the living room, sectional folder on her lap, the journals, minus one, on top.

He strode into the room, caught sight of her sitting there, and froze.

"Why don't you tell me what's going on," she said, outwardly striving for calm.

She watched him approach the sofa; the implacable expression on his face stirred dread deep within her.

He sat a few feet away and turned to face her, his jaw clenched, unable to hold eye contact with her.

"We need to contact him," she said.

"No."

Her heart sank like a stone. "Asher." She turned to face him, reached over and gripped his hand.

He pulled his hand away. "No, Maddy."

"Asher, I don't want to let her go either. I know you love her; we both love her. And it wouldn't happen right away."

"She's better off here."

"You can't know that. All the information you've gathered," she touched the file in her lap, "indicates he's a good guy with a solid, supportive family. You have all the information you need here. You've had it for days."

He refused to respond, his eyes stark, jaw clenched.

"You *know* you have to do the right thing."

His voice was cold. "And I suppose you know what that is? I won't give her up. I can give her more."

"More what, Asher? More stuff? You can't give her more love—"

"I can!" he bellowed.

"Be quiet. You'll wake her," she hissed and then coughed, and couldn't stop right away. "You can't. Asher, he's her father. It's not fair to keep them apart. You know that. This whole screwed up situation has been more unfair to him than anyone else. You have to give him a chance. You heard what the therapist said about minimizing change. Maybe he could come here and get to know her."

"If he's such a great guy, my sister wouldn't have kept him out of their lives. Who am I to mess with that? Ella's better off here. We love her."

She couldn't be hearing this right. "Asher, are you seriously considering keeping his daughter from him?"

"It's my decision."

"Where's the journal that names Ben as the father?"

He stared at her defiantly.

Something—respect? trust?—withered. In a stronger voice she said, "Where is the journal?"

"I got rid of it."

Her stomach churned. "You *what?*" she leaned forward, arms crossed over her abdomen, then stood up stiffly, knocking the file off her lap, papers spilling onto the floor with the three red books. "Asher. I won't be a party to this. This is Sterling behavior." She dashed away tears that tracked down her cheeks, a painful hole where her heart used to be.

He levered himself to his feet and gripped her shoulders. "What about me? What about my feelings for her? If I tell him, he'll take her away from me and he'll have every right," he said, bitterly. "Is that meaningless? "

"Of course not. I don't want to lose her either. There's visitation—"

"Screw visitation. Don't you see, Maddy? We can give her everything she needs. *We* can be her family."

She took two steps back, wrenching her upper arms from his grasp. This was not the man she knew and loved.

"I love you, Maddy, and together we can make a family for her."

How she'd longed to hear those words. She suspected they might even be true—it was hard to know. He'd said he was crazy about her, but he'd never used the word *love* to describe his feelings. But now? To drop that bomb in a blatant attempt to manipulate? The man standing in front of her was a chip off the Sterling Lowe block.

"Maddy, you know we can give her everything she needs, love her, care for her," he was begging now.

"Let me get this straight. Even though your research has turned up nothing untoward on this guy, nothing questionable, you *still* don't intend to tell him about Ella. Ever."

He jerked his head once, in acknowledgement.

"Asher. It's *wrong*."

He turned away.

"If you don't tell him, I will," she said.

His voice was icy, his body rigid. "It's not your decision. You aren't family. Without that journal, no one will believe you anyway. He'll look like just another guy after the Lowe fortune. You'll look like a spurned lover with an ax to grind." He turned to face her. "So help me God, Maddy, if you tell him, I'll make your life a living hell."

"It already is," she said, hoarsely, standing up. She crossed the room on trembling legs, picking up her purse from the hallway table as she continued to the front door. Once outside, she entered the code to the gate with the keypad and walked through. She couldn't even think straight. All she could hear were Asher's words reverberating in her head, his threats. A wave of guilt washed over her at the thought of leaving Ella.

She walked until she couldn't walk anymore and sat on the curb. She called Justin and gave him the cross streets.

Thirty minutes later Maddy collapsed into Justin's arms. He helped her into his car and she leaned back against the headrest, exhausted and numb. "Please take me home. I need to rest."

"What's going on?"

"I don't want you in the middle of this."

"I know how much he cares for you, Maddy. If you tell me what's wrong, maybe I can help? I've known him a long time, but I've never seen him like he's been this week. He's wrecked. Can't you at least—"

"I'll handle it, Justin," she said wearily, putting her head back against the seat.

"Do you have everything you need?" he asked, uncertainly. "Why don't you come stay with us?"

She patted her purse. "I'm good."

He looked doubtful. "But you've been living with Asher for six months."

"I'm fine, Justin. I still have plenty of stuff at my apartment." She was unaccountably weak, whether from grief or that long walk she couldn't be certain. All she knew was she needed to curl up in a ball in her bed and cry and sleep.

It was a silent ride to her apartment, where she let herself out of the car and crossed gingerly to the front door of her complex. Maddy let herself in and walked up the first flight of stairs to the landing. Once there she stopped to rest, leaning against the wall, coughing. One more flight. Exhausted beyond reason, she concentrated on putting one foot in front of the other until she was standing at her front door. It no longer looked like home. She fished out her keys from the bottom of her bag and entered her musty apartment. She wrinkled her nose as she closed the door and locked it.

Maddy got a glass of water, opened the bedroom window a crack, and moved into the tiny living room. She sat on the loveseat, still out of breath and bone tired. Odd. With all the swimming she was doing, she'd never been in better shape. She should have been able to handle a long walk and two flights of stairs. This damn cough. She took a sip of water.

It wasn't hard to find Ben Logan. His number was listed and she remembered the name of the town from the file. Still, it was early evening by the time she called him.

"Ben Logan?"

"Speaking."

"Hi. My name is Madeline Anderson. I'm calling from Los Angeles." She covered her mouth as a coughing fit overtook her.

"How can I help you?"

Maddy inhaled. "It's about Delilah Lowe."

"Yeah?"

"I understand you had a relationship."

"What's this about?" he said, tone suspicious. "Are you with the press?"

"No. I'm a nanny."

"Why do you want to know about me and Dee? That ended a long time ago."

"I know. This is going to be difficult, but…did you hear she died?"

"Yeah. Car accident right? I was sorry to hear it, but not all that surprised."

"What do you mean?"

"Well, she hung out with a bunch of partiers. She was a lot of fun but—"

"Is that why you broke up?"

He gave a short laugh. "I'm not sure you could call what we did dating—who did you say you were?"

"Her daughter's nanny."

There was a long silence.

"And…why are you calling me?"

"Because you're the father of her child."

"What?" His voice rose to a shout. Then his tone went from shocked to suspicious. "Is this a joke?"

"No. Look, I'm sure this is hard to digest, but Delilah gave birth to your baby—"

"How do you know?"

"We just found her journals. It took us a while to unpack her stuff, but when we did, she talks about you and the dates and names you as the father."

His voice shook. "Are you telling me I have an—" he paused, probably to do some calculations on dates, "—almost six-year-old child?"

"Yes."

"Ella Lowe is my daughter?"

"How do you know her name?" It was her turn to be suspicious.

He gave a sharp crack of laughter. "Please. You can't live near Vegas and not hear about what the Lowes are into. They're like royalty around here. The old man is anyway. So you are telling me that Ella Lowe is my daughter?"

"Yes."

"And I'm hearing this from the nanny?" Suspicion crept back into his tone.

"Yeah," she sighed. "Asher is having trouble coming to terms with it."

"What does that mean?"

Maddy's tone sharpened. "That means Asher and I have come to love Ella and want the best for her."

There was another long silence.

"Why isn't Asher Lowe calling? Or Sterling?"

"Ben, this isn't the easiest thing to deal with. For whatever reason, Dee didn't tell you about Ella. I do know that neither of the Lowes were aware of your existence until this week."

"You're still not telling me why I'm hearing this from you and not them."

Oh God.

"What's your name again?"

"Madeline Anderson. Maddy."

"Ella's nanny?"

"That's right."

"They weren't going to tell me, were they? Jesus!"

"Calm down, Ben. I'm sure they were…are."

"Bullshit!" Maddy could hear the fury in his tone as it sank in. "Those motherfuckers! If they think their money—"

"Listen to me, damn it. I don't blame you for being angry. Be angry with Dee, but not with Asher, and not with Sterling. I swear to God they didn't know. She never told them and believe me, they asked. *I'm* the one who found her journals. Yes, Asher is having trouble dealing with the idea that Ella's biological dad is no longer a mystery. Do you know why?"

"Why?"

"Because he loves her and cares for her and doesn't want to lose her. Are you listening to me?"

"Yeah."

"So get as angry as you want about it. Asher is a good man. He would've eventually done the right thing. And I'm beating him to the punch. He had you investigated."

"He *what*?"

"Ben, you said yourself when you met Dee and her crowd you didn't necessarily trust her judgment."

"Yeah, but—"

"Put yourself in Asher's shoes. Pretend you have a niece you love—"

"I don't have to pretend, I *have* a niece I love."

"Well then, imagine that you discover the identity of her biological father. What are you gonna do? Hand her over? Think about it."

There were a few moments of silence and then he said, begrudgingly, "Yeah. I guess I can understand that."

"Now I'm going to ask you for something."

"What?"

"I want you to keep, at the forefront of your mind, the idea that Asher and Sterling have had a terrible loss. Dee was everything to them. And to Ella. I want you to remember that Asher and Sterling love that little girl. They want to be in her life. They're good people, and she loves them. Whatever decisions you make, keep that in mind. None of this is their fault."

Ben made a noncommittal sound.

"I know you're a good guy. I read the results of the investigation."

There was a snort from the other end of the line.

"Can you do this for me?"

"I guess."

"I don't want 'I guess' I want, 'I promise, Maddy.'"

He gave a half laugh. "You sound like a teacher."

"I am."

"I promise, Maddy."

"I'm going to give you Asher's number. I'll give you Justin, his assistant's number too." Maddy rattled them off.

"Why are you telling me all of this?"

"Because Ella deserves to know her dad and you deserve to know her, and because I wasn't sure when Asher would get around to telling you. And, Ben? I've done you a favor. She's a lovely little girl. The best." Tears welled up and Maddy coughed again.

Maddy disconnected the phone call and went into the kitchen for some water. She was having a hard time catching her breath. Her chest cavity felt like it was full of glass shards. There was one more call to make before she could rest. She'd gotten the number from Ella's therapist ages ago in case of an emergency. She sat back on the couch and dialed the phone.

The tears started up again when she heard the voice on the other end of the line. "Mr. Lowe?"

"Yes?"

Maddy explained what was happening in a few short sentences. Sterling understood Asher's motivations even better than Maddy.

"Mr. Lowe, Ben's a good guy—according to all the information in that file."

"Does Asher know you notified him?"

"I told him I would."

He was silent for the count of three heartbeats. "Maddy, he won't forgive this," he said, gently.

Maddy wiped her streaming eyes. "I know."

"If you didn't have any success persuading him to do the right thing—"

"You have to try."

"Do I?" His voice was cold.

Anger surged through her. "Yes. You do. He's your son. Ella's your granddaughter. Work it out. This is a chance for you to do the right thing for a change. I tried and failed. Now it's your turn. If you really want what's best for Ella—"

"Of course I do."

"Then you know what you need to do. What's wrong with you people?"

Chapter 21

The intercom buzzed a few minutes before midnight, and Asher leaped to his feet in a surge of hope and longing. Maddy had come to her senses.

"Asher, let me in," Sterling Lowe's voice commanded over the intercom.

The bottom dropped out of his stomach, leaving him hollow, numb and vaguely nauseous.

He couldn't muster anger. Emptied of fury after Maddy left, Asher was left with sorrow and self-pity. He pushed the button to open the gates, turned off the security code, and opened the front door to wait as the motion-detecting spotlight flicked on to illuminate a black car approaching.

The limousine driver hopped out and tipped his hat to Asher. The man opened the door and helped Sterling out of the car, then went to the rear of the vehicle, popping the trunk to pull out a large suitcase.

Asher narrowed his eyes. If his dad thought he was staying, he had another think coming.

His father climbed the steps slowly.

Asher's scowl relaxed into a frown; the man was in his seventies after all. "I'll take that." Asher took the suitcase from the driver at the top of the steps, thanking him.

He waited until the driver had made his way back down the steps. "What do you want?"

"Maddy called me."

Of course she had, damn her. He followed his father across the threshold into the house. Asher shut the door forcefully and punched in the alarm code to arm it.

"Come on in." Asher led his father into the living room and switched on a light. "Can I get you anything?"

"A drink would be welcome."

Walking over to the cabinets across the room, Asher pulled out an amber bottle and two glasses. He had moved his liquor into the cabinet when Ella arrived. One of the many concessions he made to having a child in the house.

He poured them each a drink and handed one glass to Sterling, who had seated himself in the armchair. His father examined it as Asher lowered himself gingerly onto the sectional. Taking a sip, Asher savored the initial almost spicy taste, the harmonious blending of oak and honey and countless other flavors too complex for him to identify and unique to this particular fifty-year-old single-malt Scotch.

Sterling took a healthy swallow. "Balvenie," he said approvingly, raising his glass.

Asher gritted his teeth. "You were expecting Jägermeister?"

His father put the glass down on the side table with more force than was strictly necessary. "What do you want from me, son?"

What did he want from the old man? He didn't know anymore. "You're the one who showed up at," Asher glanced meaningfully at his Anonimo watch, "midnight."

"Would an apology cover it?" Sterling asked.

"Cover what?"

"My parenting? The e-mail hacking? All of it."

He sat up on the sectional, lazy affect forgotten. "What?"

"A blanket apology?" Sterling asked, his voice not quite steady, "or a specific apology for all the times I mistreated you, neglected you, underestimated you…"

Asher narrowed his eyes. *Is he mocking me?*

"I'm serious."

"How about for threatening to take Ella from my custody? You could start there."

The room was silent as his father considered him. "I think that would fall under the 'underestimated you' category," he said. "I was sure you weren't up to the task. I apologize for not understanding the depth of your character, your ability to care for and love your five-year-old niece, and change your life to accommodate hers. I don't know why I thought you incapable of that, since you took care of your sister all those years. I guess I wanted to believe it so I could keep Ella."

Asher's throat thickened and he took a slug of Scotch.

Sterling leaned forward, hands on his knees. "You must understand *now* why I was willing to do anything to make sure Ella was well taken care of. Today of all days."

"If you came here to convince me to give Ella to her father—" he said fiercely.

"I didn't. I came here to try to repair our relationship."

Asher stared. "Odd timing."

"Yes," Sterling replied.

He examined his father. Still sharp, but aging rapidly. No longer hearty, yet not quite frail. What the hell. Other than Ella, he didn't have any family left. He refused to count Jacqueline. She was worse than no family at all.

"So I apologize." Sterling pulled a sheet of paper and his reading glasses from the inside pocket of his suit jacket.

"What is that?" Asher asked.

"It's a list of my transgressions," he replied, his expression deadly serious.

Asher recoiled and raised his hands, sloshing the amber liquid in the glass. He took another desperate swallow. "Not necessary."

"I think it is," he asserted with quiet dignity. "First on the list is Jacqueline. I'm sorry I saddled you with such an unbalanced person—"

Asher snorted. "That's putting it mildly."

"—for a mother. She gave me you, and that part I can't regret."

His eyes bored into Asher, who refused to meet them. God. This was torture. Baring souls when he was emotionally raw from Maddy's defection? "Sterling, please. Not now." He didn't need this, couldn't handle this.

"It's important, son. I got custody since it was pretty clear she wouldn't take care of you. If I couldn't live with her problems, a child certainly couldn't, but I didn't behave as a father should," Sterling said formally. "I didn't make you my top priority, and I've only had the sense to be ashamed of that the last few years. Since Dee and Ella came back into my life."

This needed to stop. Right now. The raw emotions of the day combined with the alcohol made this degree of honesty intolerable. He would *not* lose it in front of his dad. His father continued down the list. "So I'm sorry for being a workaholic, a negligent and neglectful father to you and Delilah."

Asher blinked rapidly. He drained the Scotch and put the glass on the coffee table.

Breathe.

"I'm sorry I was so dismissive of your career initially."

Asher looked up at that. "Initially?"

A broad smile split his father's face. "Only initially, son. I'm a huge Spade fan."

What? Iron control kept Asher's jaw from dropping.

"I can see you don't believe me. Hmmm. What will convince you?" He brightened. "I have T-shirts!"

"Oh come on," he scoffed, "you can't expect me to believe that. You don't even wear T-shirts."

Sterling shook his head. "Oh I don't wear them. I have them under glass, lining the walls of my bedroom." He smiled, proudly.

"I usually go to a couple of shows each tour, but I only get one shirt."

Asher covered his mouth with a hand. Was he being punk'd?

Sterling rubbed his hands together. "The last one in Tokyo was amazing. That light show? Spectacular!"

"You like our music?" he said.

His father bobbed his head. "Oh yeah. Your sister dragged me to a show once, a few years before she had Ella, and I've been hooked ever since."

"You went with Dee?"

"Only once or twice when you were playing in Los Angeles."

"I don't know what to say."

"I knew you wouldn't want people to know. Wouldn't want that old press dredged up on how you wouldn't have made it without my backing. I didn't want it to be about me. But I am proud of you." He dropped his eyes back to his list. "So I've covered Jacqueline, being an absentee father, and not being supportive of your career initially. Dee was always telling me I should stop harassing you about your lifestyle." He took off his glasses and sat back. "Once everything changed for me, once Dee had Ella and I became involved in their lives, I was worried that you were taking after me."

"Taking after you?" Asher echoed, horrified.

Sterling gave him a long, sad look. "Yeah. That's what Dee told me. You don't see it. You don't see that you're a workaholic—"

No. He wasn't anything like the old man.

"—afraid to create your own family because of the mess I made of mine."

He fixed his father with a narrow-eyed glare. "Bullshit. The timing, my career—"

"Asher, you're almost forty."

"And I have a good life. Good friends."

His father nodded. "Oh, I know. I know all about Alec and Kate, Shane, Justin. You have people you love and people who love you, but have you ever gotten to that place with a woman, where you wanted to spend the rest of your life taking care of her?"

Something in his face must have given him away, because his father's expression registered surprise, followed by pity.

"Like you'd know something about that," he said hotly, though immediately he regretted his outburst. He sounded like a teenager.

Sterling leaned forward. "Just because I made bad choices about women, son, doesn't mean you have to. Is that the lesson you took from my poor choices? That it's better not to love? At least I tried."

"Did you? Did you love Jacqueline and Irene and Katherine?" Asher forced out through a stiff jaw.

"Yes, and that probably says more about me than about them. I loved all of them, maybe for the wrong reasons."

"Even Jacqueline? I find that hard to believe."

"Especially your mother." Asher watched his father's knuckles turn white on the crystal tumbler. "I'd made my first million, and there were a lot of women interested in me for my wealth. Your mother didn't care about money. She had a career and money of her own. She was beautiful, smart, accomplished, and charismatic. At least that's what I saw."

Asher's lips curled.

"It's hard to reconcile what I thought she was with who she is." He sighed. "She's disturbed, Asher. She always has been. We had a whirlwind courtship. I was madly in love with her and thought she felt the same. People tried to tell me about her problems, but I wouldn't listen. She was incredibly manipulative and highly intelligent, and I made excuses for her, tried to change my behavior to make her happy. After she gave birth to you, the writing was on the wall; there was no interest, no empathy, no maternal instinct—only manipulation and drama—and it was a lot more frightening with a child involved."

Asher eyed him, suspicious. They had never discussed his mother's problems. "She's been diagnosed?"

"Oh yeah. Personality disorder, lack of empathy, call it what you will. "

"What about the other two?"

"I married Irene because I thought she'd make a good mother. She was emotionally stable and wanted kids of her own. She insisted I give custody to Jacqueline. Back then mothers always got full custody. I wouldn't hear of it, so that ended in less than a year."

"Wow. Uh…thanks."

"You don't have to thank me, son. These were my mistakes, but I wasn't going to compound them."

"So, Katherine?"

He shrugged. "What can I tell you? She was the opposite of your mother. Contained and calm, but cold—about people, anyway. She gave everything in her to those damn horses. There was no room for anything else. I didn't try too hard to make that work, and I was no great prize."

"How can you say that?"

"Asher, I was a self-absorbed, workaholic control freak until about five years ago. I was a lost cause. And I can't be sorry about Katherine either; she gave me your sister, a gift I didn't appreciate until it was almost too late." Tears filled his eyes and he fumbled for a handkerchief.

For the second time that night Asher lost his own battle with emotion. He forestalled his tears through sheer force of will, but he covered his face with his hands.

His dad rubbed at his eyes, cleared his throat, and twisted the cloth in his hands. "I'll never be able to thank Delilah for keeping me close—no, for forcing me into her life after she got pregnant despite my initial resistance. I didn't know how to be a father or a grandfather, but Dee and Ella showed me the way, and it has been a humbling experience. So the least I can do, Asher, is share the love I feel for you the way they shared their love with me. I want to be a family with you again. I hope my apology is a first step. I know it can't happen overnight, but I'll do whatever it takes," he gave his son a hard look, "with one exception."

"And what is that?" Asher asked, but he already knew.

"We do what is best for Ella. Not you. Not me. Ella."

"And I suppose you know what that is?"

Maybe this was one long, elaborate manipulation after all.

"No. I don't," he said. "I got wind that you were investigating Ben and his family, so I did too. By all accounts, they are church-going, loving, and close-knit. No skeletons in the immediate family, though there's a cousin with a terrible meth problem."

Huh. He hadn't gotten information on the drug-addicted cousin.

His dad smiled. "I've been at this a lot longer than you, son."

"Why didn't she tell anyone who the father was?" Asher asked. "If he's such a great guy with a good family, why didn't she want Ella to know her dad?"

"I can't answer that and if her journals don't, then I guess we'll never know."

"So, now what?" Asher asked.

"Now we figure out what to do."

Chapter 22

When the cough started a week earlier, she hadn't thought much of it. It was inevitable that she would get sick—after all, she lived with a five year old and it was winter. Everyone around her seemed to be sick.

After that scene with Asher, it was no wonder she was overwrought and exhausted. But why did her body ache so? These chills were new, and she'd had enough fevers in her life to know something was seriously wrong. Breathing was increasingly difficult and painful, and she couldn't seem to stay awake. It was easier to breathe if she propped herself up on a few pillows, so that's how she'd been sleeping. Dozing really. Good thing she brought water in with her on her last trip back from the bathroom. The last time she'd tried to stand up, she almost ended up on the floor.

God, it was miserable being this sick and alone. She needed to get to her purse in the living room and make a call to her doctor. Later. She would do that later. Now she needed sleep.

It was dark when she woke again—early morning, evening, overcast? No clue. Time to get that phone. She fought the befuddlement, the pounding headache. Why was it so hot in here? Why was she back here at her apartment? Oh yeah.

Asher. Had his dad arrived? Did he hate her now? It was too tiring to think about. She tried to sit up all the way. Nope. Too dizzy. She lay back on her stacked pillows, resting, then tried again to lever herself up incrementally. Not good. She needed to call the doctor. Maybe get someone to take her there. She certainly couldn't drive in this condition. Slowly she swung her legs over the side of the bed, and slid out the side, ending up on her hands and knees on the thin, worn carpet.

Gingerly, half-crawling, she made her way into the doorway, where she rested. Had she ever been so out of breath? She coughed to try to clear her lungs.

God. Instant, sharp, debilitating pain seared her chest. She continued to make her way toward the living room, crawling down the hall, panting. Her purse was there, on the coffee table. Not far now. She made her way over to it, reached inside for her phone, its weight comforting. She pulled it out and stared. Pushed the buttons. Nothing. Dead. Panic stirred. Her charger was at Asher's. She had no landline. Maybe a neighbor?

She pulled herself up until she was leaning against the couch. A bone-jarring shudder went through her. Her hands rose to her face, hands that no longer seemed connected to her body. She was hot. Really, hot. Panting, she sat, stuporous with fatigue.

She swam up to consciousness to the sound of pounding. That damn neighbor blasting his music again. She sighed inwardly. She hated to go confront him about it, but it was really much too loud. Her walls were shaking. Hmmm. That had never happened before. She heard her name. More pounding. She tried to raise herself up from where she was, prone on the floor. No. Too weak. Ah. *Asher.* She could hear his voice now. Frantic. She tried to call out to him but couldn't do more than whisper. That sent her into a coughing fit. Paroxysms of pain swept through her and she moaned.

There was a crash, then arms encircled her aching, ultra-heated body. Asher's arms. She opened her eyes. "Asher," she whispered.

He didn't reply. He was talking to someone on his cell phone.

"Sick," she said. She looked up into his face and saw tears in his eyes. His face was taut with grief and pain and something else. Fear. His eyes were wild with it. She could hear him talking, but the words slipped away, her feverish brain unable to decipher them.

He adjusted her position until she was more upright. She gasped with pain, but she could breathe a little better. She wanted more than anything to raise her arm to stroke his beautiful, tortured face, but her body refused to cooperate as her hands laid listless against her body. Another chill swept through her. Bone-jarring like the last. He stroked her hair with gentle hands. Sometime later, through blurry eyes, she watched an endless stream of people in uniform come through her door. That was all she knew.

• • •

She lay quietly in the bed, eyes closed. Hospital room. She'd been in enough of them to know. The smell of plastic and disinfectant was unmistakable. Opening her eyes, she took in the bright morning sun. She slowly turned her head and started. Asher was lying next to her on the bed. Huh. She turned her head the other way. This was an awfully big hospital bed if two of them could sleep next to each other. She gazed over at the chair in the far corner and blinked. What on earth was her mother doing here? Her mom looked up from the book she was reading and smiled. Closing her book, she got up and came to Maddy's side.

"How are you feeling, sweetie?"

"Okay," Maddy whispered back but it came out like a croak. Her mom held a cup with a straw to her lips and she drank, gratefully.

Maddy looked over at Asher and then back to her mom.

Her mom laughed quietly.

"Oh, Maddy. You caught yourself a live one there."

"Why is the bed so big?"

"He made them get the bed they reserve for very large people; threatened to bring in his own if they didn't."

Maddy managed a small smile.

"I got here last night. You were admitted yesterday morning. You were very sick, Maddy. They were on the verge of putting you on a ventilator."

"I know, Mom, but it hit me like a ton of bricks…" she excused herself lamely.

Her mother's gaze was direct. "The doctors think the new medication you were on turned a cold into pneumonia in record time. They want to try something different. They should be in soon to talk to you about it." She looked past Maddy and frowned. "You should still be sleeping," she scolded.

Asher's deep voice answered, "Yeah, yeah," and the bed moved as he stretched.

Maddy turned her head to look at him, heard her mother's footsteps retreating and then the swish of the hospital door opening and closing.

Hot tears stung her eyes, making trails down her cheek, across her lips and chin.

Asher said something inaudible and gathered her gently to him, careful not to disturb her IV, murmuring and begging her not to cry, that it was his fault—all his fault—and it would never happen again.

"Ella?"

"She's fine. She's with my dad and Ben, but she's chomping at the bit to come see you. She was so agitated her psychologist thought it was important for her to see you—to see you were sleeping, not dead, so she came last night when you were out of it. She talked to you. I told her you could hear her and she said yeah her mom could too and—" Asher broke off and buried his face in her neck, with a keening sound, his hands clenching and releasing the rough cotton of her hospital gown spasmodically. His hands were gentle, but his body shuddered against hers.

Maddy tried her damnedest to choke down a sob but it slipped out, then another. Asher waited until the storm of weeping subsided, stroking her hair gently from her face. Even crying exhausted her. She pawed weakly at his shirt until he figured out she was trying to pull it up. He rose up on an elbow, yanked it over his head and threw it down the bed. She laid her cheek against his chest, comforted beyond reason by his familiar citrusy smell, hot skin, and the steady thumping of his heart.

She drew back as his words sank in. "With her dad? With your dad? Wait…what?"

He had pulled his phone out of his pocket and was busy texting.

"In a minute, Maddy. I promised my Dad and Ben I would contact them when you woke so Ella could come, okay?"

"Of course."

He sent the message.

"Are you comfortable?"

"Mmm." She tried to turn on her side but tethered as she was to the IV pole, it was a tough business. They finally managed, turning so she was lying on his arm and they were facing each other. Asher reached behind her for the bed controls and elevated it a smidge.

She trailed her hand with the IV attached at the wrist down his chest.

The door swung open.

"Good morning!" Maddy's rheumatologist greeted them as he entered, followed by a group of people in white coats and Maddy's mother.

Asher helped Maddy sit up. She noticed a couple of the doctors and interns trying not to stare at Asher's tattoos and failing miserably. She snickered and he looked down in surprise. He was oblivious to the stares apparently and listening intently to the plan for her care. Despite her fatigue, she concentrated on Asher's questions.

My God. He knows as much about my disease as I do. Maybe more.

"What about the investigational drug trials, the new generation of biologics?" Asher asked.

"Promising, Mr. Lowe, as is the gene therapy, but there are no guarantees. We won't consider any dramatic changes until she's more stable, and she won't be discharged for a day or two."

"I'm not staying here for the next few days," she began, her tone adamant.

"Maddy," her mother interrupted. "You'll do exactly what the doctors tell you."

Maddy set her lips mutinously.

The doctor and Asher discussed relapse, possible side effects of the new medications, rest and hydration.

Maybe he's finally starting to get the picture. Like Trey did. It must be sinking in now that he's not getting someone healthy. There's no way he can accept what the future holds for me; the hospitalizations, the flares...

"What if I get a hospital bed at home and a private duty nurse?" Asher was saying. "Can I take her with me, or would she be better off here?"

The doctor sighed. "Live-in private duty RN for the first day or two might suffice since she's coming along nicely on the antibiotics. I can make a couple of follow-up visits to your place if she's not up for coming in. A hospital bed won't be necessary if someone helps her when she needs to get in and out of bed. She may be tired and weak if she has a flare. We need to stay on top of this."

They planned the discharge for the next day, and follow-up care at home. Her doctor advised her she'd be weak for some time. That she could believe, given that she was weak as a mewling kitten.

She drifted, tuning out the drone of voices in the room.

Chapter 23

The next morning, Maddy was instructed to get out of the bed and walk the halls or the doctor wouldn't sign off on her discharge.

They were only a few steps from the room when Asher turned to face her. "Maddy, I love you."

Her heart lurched and she smiled. "I love you too, Asher."

"Will you marry me?"

She put a hand to his cheek. "No."

He glowered. "*What?* Why not?"

She continued walking slowly down the linoleum floor of the hospital corridor, IV pole in one hand. He took three steps and caught up to her, arresting her progress.

"Maddy, stop. Why won't you marry me?"

She kept her gaze on the hideous lemon-yellow, gray-flecked floor, then put her shoulders back and raised her eyes to his. The hand holding the IV pole trembled and she clenched her fingers around it. He took a step forward and wrapped his arms carefully around her. "Is it because I wouldn't tell Ben? 'Cause, admittedly, that was an epic fail. I don't know what to say other than I was in full-on panic mode. I'd like to think I would've come to my senses without you as my conscience, but I'm not sure. I need you, Maddy. And I'm sorry about everything that happened." He swallowed. "I told you I'd take care of you if you got sick and… and I didn't," he said, hoarsely.

So, that *was* it. Guilt. About Dee. About her. This wasn't about love. Well, she's give him his out.

She held herself stiffly in his arms. "It's not that, Asher." She cleared her throat to eliminate the tremor in her voice, leaned away, and continued down the hall. "I don't want to get married."

He reached out for her arm again; she wrenched it away.

"Maddy, please."

"You can let go of the guilt. Okay? I know you feel bad about what happened. All of it—"

"You think I'm asking you to marry me because I feel *guilty*?" He stepped in front of her and raised an arm. "Hold up."

"No, not exactly," she hedged.

"And I'm not asking because I want to keep Ella either. I mean, I do want to keep Ella, but I think I'm going to have to settle for…well, I'll lose custody. There's no doubt about that. Ben is adamant and I know the court would never—"

"No, it's not that."

"Then what? Jesus. I love you." He raked his hands through his hair, and for the first time she saw the lines of stress and fatigue etched into his face, his hair, run through too many times with anxious hands. Had he even been home to shower?

She pressed her lips together and blinked rapidly but managed to keep her tone even. "There's no cure for what I have, Asher."

He frowned. "I know that."

"I'm sick, Asher."

Now he just looked annoyed. "Yeah. I know."

She scowled. "Asher, I have a chronic, progressive illness. I have fatigue, pain, mobility problems—"

"I know. I live with you, sleep with you. You think I can't tell when you're tired and in pain? You may have been able to hide it from me early on, but not anymore. Not since I fell in love with you."

Her heart rate accelerated at his words. It was difficult to draw a breath but it had nothing to do with the pneumonia. "I've been pretty healthy since we met, but I have flares, complications—hospitalizations. This is life long, Asher."

"So fucking what?"

"There's no *cure*. I'm not going to get better, but I will get worse—"

"So? I mean, yeah, so we'll deal with it."

Tears filled her eyes and her hand went to her mouth. "You say that now, but it will get bad as time goes on. It's the nature of the disease."

He looked furious; temper leapt in those golden eyes, now red-rimmed with fatigue.

She took a step back. For someone with legendary control, he sure did lose his temper with her a lot.

He followed, his hands closed like manacles on her upper arms. His arms shook as he bent, looming over her. "You think I care? You think I fucking *care* about that? You *know* me. You know I love you. Maddy, I'd do anything for you. *Anything*. I never loved another person the way I love you. Before I met you, I had Dee and Spade, and a handful of good friends. I thought I had it all." He rolled his eyes. "And then you and Ella came into my life and flipped it upside-fucking-down. I don't know what is where anymore—all I know is I'm crazy in love with you and I *will* spend the rest of my life with you. In sickness, and in health. Bring it."

Maddy stared, tears running down her cheeks.

He reached out a trembling hand and stroked it gently down her cheek, clearing tears that were making a salty procession to her mouth.

"I'll take care of you," he said, "if you get sick. We're in this together, Maddy."

She tilted her head. Longing surged through her as she shook her head. "But Asher, that's just it, I don't want to need you more—and I *don't* want you to have to take care of me."

He gazed, unblinking, into her eyes, a slight quirk to his lips. "Oh, Maddy, don't you know? I'll always be the one who needs you more. You were whole when we met, and I'm just figuring it out, thanks to you and Ella, but I still have a helluva long way to go. I need you to get there."

He dug around in his pocket and went down on one knee.

Maddy looked down into his distinctive amber eyes, her vision blurred by tears.

"I love you, Maddy. Will you please marry me?"

"Yes." she croaked, then cleared her throat, coughing. "I love you, too."

He slipped the ring on her finger.

She plucked at his shoulder to bring him to his feet, then got a good look at the ring. Aghast for a moment, her sense of humor kicked in and she laughed until she coughed, leaning against him.

It wasn't just large. It was hideous and large.

"Oh, God. Asher! It looks like a Superbowl ring." She covered her mouth with her hand. "And here I thought you had such good taste."

He grinned. "I do. But since I haven't left the hospital, I had to get my dad to pick one up. His poor taste is legendary. Wait till you see his house."

"Can't wait," she said, reaching up to kiss him.

Epilogue

Among the exclusive club of rock's greatest frontmen, Asher Lowe tops the list. His rarified status isn't just based on number-one hits or platinum album sales, though Spade has plenty of those. No, it's because he has that rare mixture of style, charisma, onstage exuberance, good looks—plus the vocal chops and guitar skills to back it up. Lowe has been in the news a lot over the past two years due to the death of his sister, his marriage, and a single, "Home," that broke every sales record in alternative rock. In a candid conversation, Asher Lowe talks to Player Magazine *about love, making his mark on music, and finding himself.*

So why is Spade doing a residence in Vegas and four shows a week? Your father has always lived there, but you've avoided the place. You've gone on record saying you love L.A. and would never leave California. Why no tour?

Never say never, man. I violated a lot of my rules these last few years. [*laughs*] But seriously, Spade has been on the road for the last two decades and we were burnt. This way we can perform for our fans without having to uproot our lives. Most of the band live in L.A. and fly in. I'm here in Vegas with my wife so we can be close to my dad, my niece, and her dad's family. We may head back to L.A. at some point. I miss California, but it's a short flight.

Your exploits with women were the stuff of legend and fantasy. And now you're married?

Yeah. What magazine is this again? [*laughs*] I was that guy for a lot of years. I've always been respectful of women but very open to having a good time. [*shrugs*] Hey, it was all good—the partying, the women, the road—but things changed when my niece came to live with me. I realized that the life I wanted included family. And a lover who cares more about what's inside my head than inside my pants. Before Maddy, I never understood why someone in my line of work would choose to settle down with just one person. And I think that's why Spade's single "Home" resonates with so many. Those of us who have found home would kill or die or change to keep it.

There was a lot of speculation about your wife's health and the fact that she was your nanny.

Maddy's very open about her health issues. In fact, she's the reason I agreed to this interview. Spade is doing a benefit concert in L.A. on November 3rd for the Arthritis Foundation. My wife suffers from rheumatoid arthritis, an inflammatory type of arthritis and autoimmune disorder that affects the joints; a disease that affects nearly one percent of the nation's adult population. It's a painful, chronic, progressive illness. There are treatments but no cure, and some of the most effective medications are very expensive. And yes, I hired her as my niece's nanny and fell hard. I didn't believe in love like that before I met Maddy—despite Spade songs to the contrary. [*laughs*]

What does the future hold?

I had a birthday recently. When I went to blow out the candles, I realized I didn't have anything to wish for. I have Maddy and my Dad, Ella and her dad's family, great friends and Spade. Hey, it's not perfect. Loving someone who struggles with pain and fatigue on a daily basis, and being helpless when that person suffers, is tough. But I want to be there. Every day. There are a lot of good times and more to come because Maddy and I will be welcoming a baby into our family in a few weeks. It's an incredible life, and I'm the luckiest guy on the fucking planet.

About the Author

Fueled by black jelly beans and Pinot noir, Rachel Cross writes contemporary romance that rocks. She lives in coastal California with her surfer/pilot husband and two daughters. Her past includes stints as a firefighter, paramedic, clinical manager, and *Weekly World News* tabloid model.

Read more about her at *www.readrachelcross.com*, on Twitter @ReadRachelCross, and on her Facebook page: *www.facebook.com/pages/Rachel-Cross/116558055203658?ref=hl*.

A portion of the proceeds from the sales of this book will go to the Arthritis Foundation *www.arthritis.org*.

A Sneak Peek
from Crimson Romance

Rock Her by Rachel Cross

Chapter 1

She's okay, Mom.

As her feet pounded out a rhythm on the hard packed sand, her mother's tarnished locket with its shiny new chain bounced on her chest. She held it briefly before sliding it back under her shirt.

Kate took the first mile slowly, warming up her legs as she ran the sloping path from her two-bedroom guesthouse to Mar Vista Beach. The surf was small. Nevertheless, two surfers were offshore trying to catch waves. Her only other company was a beachcomber or runner, barely visible in the distance. Heading south to the point break, she picked up her pace.

All those years making meals for two, checking homework, cheering Emma on in life and sports; it all came to an abrupt end when Kate put Emma on the plane four weeks ago. Her sister, attending college three thousand miles away. Was it possible to have empty-nest syndrome at twenty-five?

The dog—Zack, according to his collar—was a welcome and familiar sight at this beach. While his owner surfed the break, Zack waited patiently with his tennis ball. Kate bent to pick up the soggy ball and pitched it into the waves. Zack retrieved it as she continued running. He chased her for a few steps, hopeful.

Some mornings Kate was so lost in her thoughts she wouldn't have noticed if her path took her straight through a nude sunbathing area. But today everything distracted her, the blue gray of the Pacific, the pelicans diving in the wide gap between the two surfers waiting for waves, and the beauty of home.

Kate watched one of the surfers, Zack's owner. She'd seen him numerous times on her runs, sitting, his board perfectly angled to see the incoming waves. Fall was calm, unlike winter when storms could bring waves twenty feet high to this part of the

California coast. Growing up in Cielito, almost everyone surfed something at some point. Longboard, shortboard, bodyboard, stand-up paddleboard—there was a board for everyone. She had spent countless hours surfing, swimming, and bodyboarding at this very beach. Now? Despite the heat her run generated, she gave a small shiver. The ocean was cold, even with a wetsuit. She'd take a heated swimming pool any day over that sixty-degree water.

The same two surfers were still in their spots as she made her way back down the beach. She threw the ball for Zack again and lifted a hand to his owner. He sat on his board waiting for the next set of waves, but he raised a hand in return.

She looked out to the other surfer, some fifty yards from Zack's owner. Not there. Odd. He was there a second ago; his board was still there. She picked up her pace, staring intently at the space where the surfer should've been. Nothing. No one on the beach either. What the hell? Why was his surfboard still sitting, fins up, as if anchored...

Oh no. Oh my God.

Functioning solely on adrenaline, she raced to the water, barely pausing to toe off her shoes in the icy surf before running into the sea. Numb within seconds from the cold, she took one deep breath and plunged under the first breaking wave.

The sea was calm as she struck out for the board with a frantic freestyle stroke. Panic lent her speed. She reached the surfboard in moments. She took another deep breath—not easy since exhaustion from the run, coupled with the cold Pacific, left her damn near hyperventilating.

She dove into the murky water under the board, hands searching for and finding the flexible rubber tube, the leash, which normally attached a surfer to his board. She hoped and prayed it was still attached. She yanked it. Heavy. She followed the leash down, deeper until icy flesh brushed her fingers. His ankle. *Thank God.*

She grabbed for him, barely able to see his black-clad body in the dark water. She ran her hands up his ankle, past his leg and hip, until she reached his chest. She wrapped one arm under his wetsuit-covered armpit, then kicked with all her strength, finally breaking the surface.

Gasping for breath, legs pumping, she struggled to pull the unconscious man's limp head out of the water. *He weighs a ton!*

She looked up to see the other surfer, Zack's owner, in front of her. He rolled off his board without a word, turned it upside down, fins up, draped the man's arms over the board, and with considerable exertion, levered it up and over. The board flipped, distributing the unconscious man's torso onto the middle of the board. He unleashed the man from his shorter inverted surfboard, which pitched on the waves. With the board in front of him, he started for shore, Kate in his wake. The dark-haired man fought the beach break, barely managing to keep the board upright. He grunted as he dragged the drowning victim off the board, then turned him face up, just beyond the water's edge. Kate all but crawled out of the water on his heels. Muscles cramped from the cold, she hobbled over to the lifeless body. Every second counted with a drowning victim.

"I'm an RN," she said, jaw clenched from nerves and cold.

"Can you handle this?" the surfer asked.

"Yes. But we need a phone to call nine-one-one."

He glanced down the beach where a jogger was headed toward them. The surfer took off after him at a dead run.

Kate examined her patient from head to toe. He was young, really young. That made heart issues less likely. His wetsuit didn't indicate damage to the material or blood, so whatever was wrong with him, it wasn't a shark attack. She felt for a pulse and listened for breaths. He had a pulse. Good.

She adjusted his head to open his airway, listened, and felt for breath. Nothing. She readjusted his head. Still nothing. With her lips to his she started mouth-to-mouth resuscitation, her body moving on autopilot through the steps of breathing for him. She needed paramedics if this guy was going to have any chance, and she needed them now.

"Breathe, damn it!" She rechecked his pulse. Weak, but still there. That was something. She put air into his cold, still body. She looked up at the approach of the tall surfer. She could hear enough of his side of the conversation to realize he was communicating with the emergency dispatcher. He must've gotten a phone from that person down the beach.

"He's still unconscious, unresponsive. I have a pulse but no respirations." She breathed again. "How far out is the medic?" Even she could hear the frantic edge to her voice. *Calm down.* She rubbed wet hair out of her eyes and continued to work, the stillness interrupted only by the surfer's terse responses to the nine-one-one dispatcher.

Finally, shrieking sirens broke through the quiet on the beach. She closed her eyes and ushered up thanks. When she opened them, she was gazing directly into the bright blue eyes of the neoprene-clad man kneeling across from her.

"I'd take over, but…"

"You can't," she said between breaths. "Unless you're trained?"

"No. The dispatcher told me to let you handle it, until you become unable."

She grimaced. "I'm able. God, they need to hurry!"

To find out more about *Rock Her*,
visit *www.crimsonromance.com*.

Also Available

In the mood for more Crimson Romance?
Check out *The Wicked Bad* by Karyn Gerrard
at *www.crimsonromance.com*.

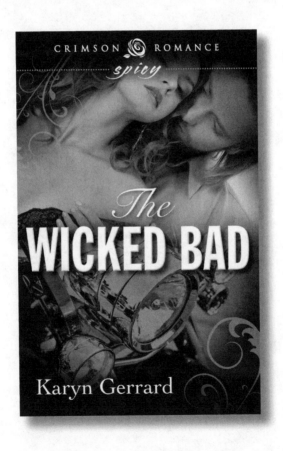